The Black Butterfly

Peace at Last

By

Cornelia Smith

The Black Butterfly Peace at Last
Copyright © 2015 by Cornelia Smith
All Rights Reserved

This is a work of fiction. Names, characters, businesses, places, events and incidents are either the products of the author's imagination or used in a fictitious manner. Any resemblance to actual persons, living or dead, or actual events is purely coincidental.

No part of this publication may be reproduced, distributed, or transmitted in any form or by any means, including photocopying, recording, or other electronic or mechanical methods, without the prior written permission of the publisher, except in the case of brief quotations embodied in critical reviews and certain other noncommercial uses permitted by copyright law.

www.thebookplug.com

Other Titles by Cornelia Smith

1. Sleeping in Sin: The Lesson
2. Sleeping in Sin: The Revenge
3. Sleeping in Sin: On The Run
4. Sleeping in Sin: With A Stranger

- The Swirl: A haunted Crave
- The Real Friends of Atlanta
- The Black Butterfly: A Damaged Soul
- The Black Butterfly: A Lost Soul

Available Now!

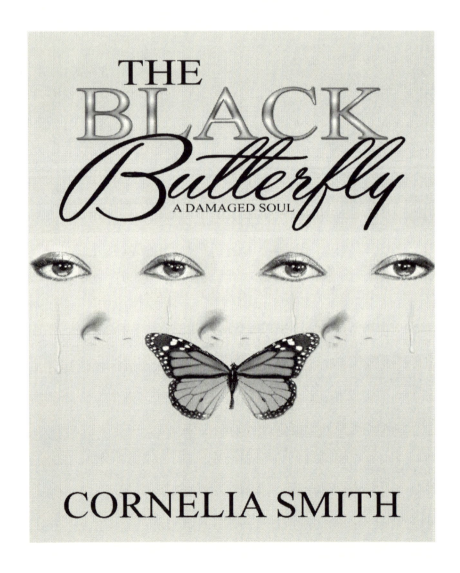

Available Now!

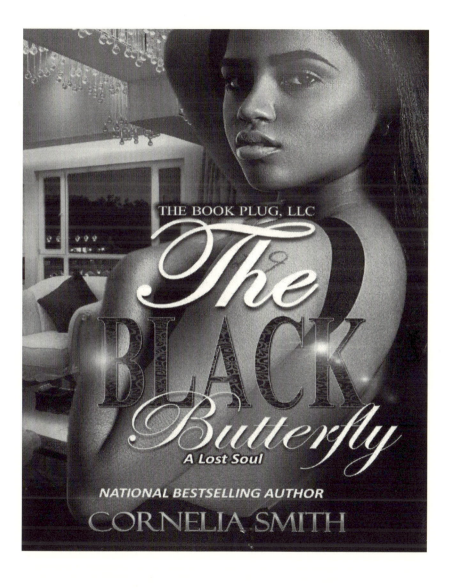

1

Shy changed her wig more often than her undergarments. She was a brunette in the early morning light, soft curls falling to her shoulders. Before noon she wore a blonde bob and by evening time she was all red, straight hair cascading to her lower back. She ironed out the wrinkles in her little black dress looking herself up and down in the mirror as she prepared for her second date of the day. Becoming a house wife was her real goal. She was only in college for the cover up.

Shy learned from her daddy, that a man seemed to like the sound of a woman being independent but liked her to be dependent upon him more. And Shy was down for the traditions. Just as soon as she found the right man to love and spoil her, she was going to marry him. But first she had to kiss a couple of frogs first.

Quickly, Shy sprayed on Beyoncé *Heat* perfume at the sounds of taps on her room door.

"Coming!" As soon as Shy opened the door she was rushed by a man in a mask. He roughly pushed opened her dorm room door and shut it behind him.

"Don't make a sound bitch!" Shy, did the exact opposite. She was in a dorm room. Someone was bound to hear her. At least that's what she assumed would happen before the beast knocked her lights out with one blow to her head......

Twenty-minutes had passed, and Shy had finally opened her eyes.

"Tell me where your roommate at, BITCH!"

"I don't know where she at. She's not my roommate anymore!" Shy mumbled as the beast circled the desk chair she was bound to. She sat there and cried in agony, the ropes were tied so tight that they stopped her circulation. The masked intruder grew frustrated and struck the beauty across her temple with the butt of his gun, splitting her flesh opened. Blood trickled down her face as she cringed in pain.

"Tell me! Where does she stay now?! It's got be somewhere around here. This damn school isn't that big, where you don't run into her nowhere." He screamed as he ripped the ski mask off his head, tired of waiting for a response. His face was uglier than a burn patient; skin crumbled up like wrinkle paper, teeth yellow and surprisingly, he was a Caucasian man with an Russian accent. He knew his target was somewhere close and he hated coming this far and leaving empty handed. Plus, after Shy, the campus was going to be on alert.

Shy just cried in pain and never answered the prowler question, frustrating him to the brink of rage.

"If you don't tell me what I want to know, I'm going to blow your pretty little brains all over this wall. The monster said as he pointed the gun at the young lady's head. He waited for a response, only to get nothing from her except more tears. He knew that he didn't have a lot of time before someone knocked on the door. It was a dorm room. There was always traffic, he assumed. He had already searched the room from top to bottom and came up with no clues about his target where about.

He slapped Shy, taking her silence as disrespect. He put his gun on his waist and wrapped his hands around her neck and squeezed with all his might. He watched her ace turn blush red. She squirmed but there wasn't much she could do because of the ropes restraining her limbs. The intruder thought about how she had blatantly disrespected his power and wanted to see her die. He didn't need her alive anyway if she wasn't going to tell him what he needed to know. In his twisted mind, it would be payback for undermining his authority. He continued to squeeze her throat until the squirming stopped and her eyes stared into space... at nothing. She was dead.

Finally, he loosened his grip, letting her chin fall into her chest. He breathed heavily and stepped back from the Shy lifeless body. He took one more look around the room and still, nothing. Quietly, he slipped out the room with his head held down, face hiding behind his Savannah state cap.

As Brody drove down the highway, Shaniya yawned and then kicked her feet up on the dashboard. She glanced down at the clock on the dashboard. She hated being out so late but the game had went in over time when the game got tied up. Both Savannah state and Georgia Southern was to good teams. Shaniya had tried to get her captain to let them go home but she said they had to stay and she glad she did because the girls had challenge them to a dance off.

College was everything Shaniya thought it would be. She used to look at Drumline just to see the girls dance and she had secretly wished she could go but she knew her grades wasn't the brains, Skylar was, and her momma didn't necessarily have the money, she was a stripper barely making ends meet for them to eat.

When Kerry and Bryan had broken the news to her that they were going to pay for her to go to college, she didn't know what to do. She screamed for what seemed like days, and when she was done crying, she promised to repay them by graduating.

Brody played on basketball team and he was madly in love with Shaniya. He had only gone to the football game to see Shaniya dance and to keep the Q-dogs off her. As

Brody parked the car, Shaniya gathered up her dance bags and her books. She hadn't been to her dorm all weekend. Brody wanted her to stay with him since his roommate had gone home for the weekend. As soon as they were out the car, they rushed for the building. Running from the cool breeze and low temperatures.

"Hold up, wait a minute." Shaniya said as she saw the crowd swarming around her old room.

"What's going on here?" She asked breaking her way through the crowd.

"It's Shy!" One of the girls who stayed in the dormitory building said.

"What's wrong with Shy?" Shaniya screamed as she made her way into her old room. As soon as she walked into the room she noticed Shy stretched out on the bed. One of the girls tried CPR on her but there was no hope. She was gone.

"Who did this?" Shaniya cried out.

"I think it must've been a robbery attempt." Brody said as he walked around the room.

"Don't touch nothing, Brody. We are waiting on the police to come." Shy new roommate Tonya said.

"I can't believe this, shit!" Shaniya heart dropped when she noticed the way the room had been torn up. It was if a tornado had run through it. The bed was flipped over, and the drawers were pulled out and emptied onto the floor. *This was no robbery, they were looking for something.* Shaniya thought as she pulled Brody out the room to the side.

"*This was no robbery, come on we got to go.*" She whispered aggressively into his ear.

"What are you talking about?" Brody whispered back.

"Come on, I'll tell you later. I got to go call my aunt." Hurriedly, Shaniya and Brody disappeared out of sight. Shaniya didn't want to go to her room, so she led Brody to their room instead.

"What's going on Shaniya?" Brody asked as soon as they were alone in his room.

"I'll explain later." She answered as she paced the room back and forth with her IPhone pasted to her ear.

"Come on, answer!" Shaniya was on her second call and still no one was answering the phone. It wasn't until she called the firth time that she got a response.

"Aunt Kerry!" she yelled into the phone.

"Shaniya?"

"Aunt Kerry, are you sleep?"

"What you think, Shaniya? It's eleven something!"

"I think he found me." She whispered into the phone, walking into the corner where Brody couldn't hear her.

"What are you talking about?"

"You know who?" Shaniya answered before she broke down into tears.

"Shaniya, calm down. Where is Brody?"

"He's right here." Shaniya answered in between sniffles.

"Give him the phone, please." Shaniya tried to wipe her tears away before walking away from the corner.

"My aunt wants to talk to you." She said as she handed him the phone.

"Hey, Ms. Kerry?"

"Hey, Brody. I need a favor."

"Yes, sure. Anything." Brody feared Kerry. She had showed him a trick that she would do to his balls if he had ever done Shaniya harmed.

"Can you bring Shaniya home for me?"

"Right now?" He quickly, asked.

"No, early tomorrow morning. I don't want yaw out on the road right now. In the meantime let her stay at your room, please and thank you."

"Sure. I can do that." Brody hung up the phone and Shaniya ran and tucked herself into his arms.

"I'm scared, Brody."

"You're going to be fine. Aint nothing about to happen to you here."

2

Kerry had been having a fantastic pity party for herself for three days straight. In a couple of hours, it ends. She couldn't let Shaniya know that she was going through some things. Primary reason, she didn't know exactly what she was going through. She just didn't feel like herself anymore. It was like her identity was slipping through the cracks. She didn't know who she was anymore. Her life as she knew it was all about the kids and Bryan. She had lost the independent woman she once was somewhere between *I Do* and *pushing out a baby*.

She's suffering in bed because she feels worthless. It's like her soul hurt. She wasn't sure how the Hennessey was going to help but she sipped from the bottle hoping the poison would lift her spirit. She couldn't tell if she was drunk or not, but Shaniya and Brody would be arriving in a couple of hours and she had to brace herself. She stared blankly at the TV, watching Halle Berry play a character name Niecey. Niecey was passionate about making it big and she convinced her friend to fly out to California with her to pursue their dreams. "Where my friends like that?" Kerry mumbled before B.A.P.S went to commercial.

Get up Kerry, pull it together. She thought. She stared at the television and only to watch yet another commercial about a cure for suffering from something. She took another tiny sip of her Hennessey instead of a long slow one. "Yes, I love my child, yes, I'm thankful to have my nieces with me, yes, I love my husband, but I also want a life for me. That's right, I want something that screams Kerry. I want my own job. Maybe, I want to go to school. I don't know, I just know I want something that belongs strictly to Kerry." Kerry talked to herself, lying flat onto her back, staring up at the ceiling.

"I know things happens for a reason. So, this time at home is probably time for to reevaluate what I like doing. As of this moment, I have yet to think of anything that would lift my skirt. So, I'll just take all this at home time to figure that out." Kerry rolled back onto her stomach and the commercials was stead of rolling. This time she was staring at a Viagra commercial. Which reminded her, "Shit, I haven't given my husband no sex in two weeks or has it been three? Damn, I don't know. Shit!" She murmured.

"What is going on?!" she blurted out at the television. This is like the third or fourth or filth commercial for antidepressant she's saw today. She had been noticing just how many prime-time ads all seemed to be pushing pills for whatever might pain peoples. Kerry felt there were so many commercials for antidepressants that maybe she was missing out on the new trend. Now she'd start to wonder if she should get a few months' supply of Cymbalta to help her wade through her rough patch, although she knew she didn't make a good candidate for depression. Feeling sorry for herself took too much time and energy. She was slowly discovering how hard it was to do nothing. Three days was long enough to be down.

"Tomorrow I'm going to hit the gym. I'm going to sweat out every drop of despair and booze." She mumbled out before taking another sip from the bottle. Finally, Halle is back on the screen, busting some of her best moves for an audition. Looking like the sexiest hood chic in Hollywood.

"I love this movie. You go Halle!" Kerry blurt out. After a few more minutes, Kerry realize she's not out the bed yet. It's almost noon and she'd been stuck in the spot all morning. The kids were at Bryan's mothers house and Bryan was gone to work. She had the house just like she liked it; all to herself. Finally, she jumped up out of bed fetching the bathroom and then suddenly, there's knocks on the door.

"Uh-oh. Shaniya's here. Kerry hear her knocking hard. She never rang the doorbell like normal peoples. "Ghetto ass," Kerry thought on her way down the stairs.

"I'm coming little girl, hold your horses!" Kerry felt a little light headed as she made her way down the stairs. Before she opened the door, she pressed her cheek against it: "Don't say a word about how bad I look, because I haven't been in any mood for dressing up, okay?"

"Okay! Open the door, please, Aunt! I have to go to the bathroom, badly!" As soon as the door is opened, Shaniya dashed right past Kerry in very tight denim jeans.

"Shaniya, have you gained weight?"

"Are you blind? No, I haven't!" she yells from behind the door.

"I think you have. Your ass looks thicker. You better not be pregnant, I know that!"

"Don't start with me, Aunt." Shaniya came out the restroom and stood in the hallway with her arms crossed.

"I'm not ready for more kids right now."

"You better not be." Kerry snapped.

"Oh, hey Brody. How have you been?" Brody stood in the living room like a scared soul.

"Hey, Ms. Kerry."

"You can sit down, Bryan should be here in a minute to keep you company." Nervously, Brody sat down slowly onto the sofa.

"Where is Bryan, on a Saturday?" Shaniya flopped down the sofa next to Brody.

"The law firm had a charity event today."

"And you didn't go with him? That's not like the "Good Wife" I know." Shaniya had no idea the affect her joke had on Kerry.

"Nope! I'm clocked out." Kerry replied.

"Where is everybody? Where is the kids and Skylar?" Shaniya jumped up from the sofa and headed towards the kitchen.

"I got rid of everyone, so we could talk." Kerry lied as she followed Shaniya into the kitchen. She sent everyone away because she was tired of the noise. She wanted to hear non-stop silence. It was the same reason she didn't accompany Bryan at his Charity event. She just wanted to be along.

"You sounded worried over the phone. So, I sent the kids with Claire and Skylar is out with her friends somewhere." Shaniya took a deep breath and then exhaled.

"You right, they probably shouldn't be here. I just miss Khloe so much and little Bryan."

"There be back tonight, buts what's going on?" Shaniya looked out the kitchen and into the restroom to see what Brody was doing; he was staring blankly at the television like a deaf statue.

"My roommate was killed, last night."

"She was killed? I thought they just robbed the room." Kerry asked.

"No! They killed her and trashed the room but none of her things was missing. Not her money, no clothes, nothing of value." Shaniya whispered looking back and forth from the living room to the kitchen.

"Okay, that doesn't mean it has anything to do with you Shaniya. is serving time all the way in Jamaica, Shaniya. Jamaica!" Kerry held back her tone so that Brody wouldn't hear her, but she didn't hold back her irritable expression.

"Okay, if you say so." Talking to her aunt, always relieved her stress. She knew now what she what she didn't know years ago; Kerry loved her family more than words could describe and if she wasn't worried, Shaniya figured, she shouldn't be either.

"Yes, I say so. Just watch who you talk to. Keep your circle small and but stay around a crowd. If you get what I'm saying?"

"Yes, I get you. That's why I'm always under Bryan like winter time."

"Yeah, keep him around. And don't go nowhere at night by yourself."

"Hell, I don't even go nowhere by myself in the morning or afternoon." Shaniya joked.

"Well, you should be fine because I honestly don't think we have nothing to worry about. is stashed away in a Jamaica prison. We're good, trust me! Now, let me go get dressed. Bryan is bringing over one of his old school friends tonight. He and Kelsey want to play charades."

"Oh, that should be fun. Count me and Brody in."

3

Skylar had heard about the football team parties but attending them was a completely different story. The team went all out for the victory celebration. North Atlanta high had just won their homecoming against their rivalry school, Grady and the kids were lit. It was no club in Atlanta more jumping. Initially, Skylar had told her boyfriend she wasn't going to go but Dontae wasn't taking no for an answer, anymore.

He was the quarterback and one of the most popular boys in school and he could have any girl he wanted. Skylar had better been thankful he was checking for her, at least that's how Dontae viewed it. He wasn't going to keep letting Skylar disc him like he was a lame, when in reality she was closer to being a square than he was.

The party was the wildest shit Skylar had ever seen. Sex and drinking for days. Girls were ducked off in the corner with boys all over the house. Some couples were kissing, others were drinking, and some was smoking weed. The girls that weren't indulging in sex, pot or drinks was on the dance floor twerking far better than strippers could ever.

Dontae and Skylar had been upstairs in his room away from the party for over twenty minutes. He had entertained Skylar with stories about his trophies and then about his daddy who played professionally for the NFL, trophies. Skylar was glad she had decided to come to the party after all. She and Dontae had seemed to be growing closer. And then suddenly, what she thought wasn't on his mind; sex. With time became very clear, that it was.

He made 'sexual' comments, jokes, gestures, and Skylar ignored the signals. Jumping up from the bed to look at old family pictures hanging around. He then began to accidentally brush up against her from behind cornering her to the wall. When she had finally made her way back to the bed, he began to linger his hand longer than it usual was around her waist.

"What's the matter? Are you scared?" He asked before thrusting his tongue down her throat. The kiss was everything the romantic movies made them out to be, but Skylar knew if she didn't stop it, the kiss would quickly graduate to the real deal and she wasn't ready for that type of fireworks yet. So, she quickly pushed Dontae away.

"It's not that I'm scared. I'm just not ready, Dontae. We're still in school. And I'm not trying to go down that road and get all caught up. You know?" Dontae rubbed his chin, trying his hardest to keep his patients. He jumped up off the bed to pull her back into the room. She was charging for the door.

"Wait, don't go. I'm not trying to rush you. It's just, I like you and well, I got needs. I'm not a virgin, so I get the urge. And I don't want to hook up with nobody else." Gently, Dontae pulled Skylar in closer to him. She inhaled the scent of his cologne and thought, *it should be a crime for a man to smell this damn good. Shit!*

"I don't want to rush you, Skylar but you just so damn beautiful to me." His beard glazed her cheeks, and he brushed his lips on hers. His hand traveled the distance from her shoulders to her buttocks. He gripped her firm ass, massaging it in his hands. Timidly, she pulled away from him, her knees knocking against each other.

"Tell me, you want it." He whispered into her ear as he slowly walked her back over to the bed.

"Tell me, you're mines. Say it!" He demanded before thrusting his tongue back down her throat. Skylar laid flat on her back with Dontae between her legs. Every hormone in her body was raging. He felt good between her, but she never not once changed her mind about not giving it up. In fact, she knew what he didn't know and that was, she wasn't going to let him get farther then kissing her breast. Just as he began kissing her breast gently, a sudden *BOOM* interrupted them, At the door.

"Really, Dontae?!" Dontae ex-girlfriend Shanika screeched out.

"Man, chill out with all that ghetto shit, for real!" Nervously, Skylar button back up her white blouse. The whole party was standing outside the room and stuffed in the door way as if Shanika had announced she was about to bring drama to Dontae way before getting to the room.

"How you up in here kissing up on this bitch when you were just with me the other night, talking about how you love me and all that?" Skylar attempted to walked pass Shanika in hopes she could avoid the increasing drama.

"Bitch! I knew all that good girl shit was just an act. Talking about you're a virgin and shit. Bitch, you're a hoe just like the rest of the groupies!"

"I am a virgin. No lie in that. It's not my fault you been giving it up since you were ten." Just as the party igged on the fight with a, *OOOH*! Shanika struck Skylar. With all the tension between them, she didn't see the hit coming. She didn't believe Shanika would really hit her. A sudden gush of pain jolted throughout Skylar's body. Her stomach ached, her arms lost tension and her legs began to weaken.

"She will not get the better of me," she thought as she dropped to the ground. Her tongue was soaked in the taste of blood. Bruised and winded, with a leg in agony, she tried to grab Shanika's foot and pull her to the ground, but she just started kicking Skylar in her face. Her head was pounding. She gave up on fighting because it only caused Shanika to hit her harder, so instead she bald up on the floor. Praying someone, Dontae anybody would feel sympathy and break it up.

After five long minutes, Dontae finally did what he should have the moment the fight started, he grabbed Shanika up off Skylar.

"You are tripping, man! Get out my house with all this bullshit girl." He said with a smirk on his face. The whole situation had him tickled. He got a thrill out the girls fighting for him.

"You better get that bitch out of here before I beat her ass to sleep." Dontae did just that, he grabbed Skylar by the arm and walked her to the car. The two disappeared in the wind as he pushed the fast-yellow Mustang to its limit.

4

Chante smiled at Bryan in a way that never meant good things, and unintentionally his face was washed with desire. She rolled back her shoulders and observed as his eyes were drawn downward. She tossed her amber hair and glanced his way, before she drew her next clue on the board.

"Bitch, are you going to draw the damn clue or flirt?" Finally, Kerry had exploded. All night Chante had been flirting with Bryan and everybody knew it but him. He assumed she was her regularly out going self.

"Oh, no! Kerry, I'm not flirting with Bryan. Girl, we always play like this." Kelsey looked over at her man, Joc and with fear in her eyes. She knew how rowdy Kerry could get and she knew the anger had been boiling all night. She was surprised Bryan was even playing around with fire the way he was.

"Girl, your ass been flirting all night but it's cool because he seems to be enjoying the attention. Just draw the next clue so we can get this game over with already." Bryan set up on the sofa, "Kerry?"

"Don't fucking Kerry me Bryan. Just save that shit. In fact, you know what? Everybody get the fuck out!" Kerry snapped.

"Party over!" Kerry began scooping up the trashy plates of food from around the house, tossing them in the small Wal-Mart shopping bag.

"What's wrong with you Kerry? Why are you acting like this?" Bryan questioned as he followed behind Kerry around the living room.

"What do you mean, why she is acting like this?" Shaniya jumped up from the sofa and blurted out.

"You and Miss thang over there being flirting all night like she doesn't even exist or something. You lucky we aint beat that bitch ass yet." Nervously, she gathered up her things.

"I'm sorry if I've made you feel some type of way. That wasn't my intention. I would…" Kerry interrupted Chante, holding her hand up signaling her to stop talking.

"Listen, you don't owe me anything. You're just being a woman. I'm only married to one person and he's the only that's got some explaining to do." Before Bryan could respond Skylar barged into the house and all eyes fixated on her bruised face. She was dripping blood. She didn't bother wiping herself down in the car because she was too embarrassed and angry with Dontae.

"What the hell happened to you?!" Kerry blurted out, instantly forgetting her problem with Bryan.

"I don't want to talk about it!" Skylar yelled back as she sped walked to her room.

"Let me go see what's going on with her." Quickly, Shaniya chased behind Skylar and before she could make it to her room, Skylar slammed the door behind her and locked it.

"Skylar, come on. Open the door." Shaniya pleaded out.

"No! Just leave me alone, Shaniya. Please!"

"What happened, Skylar?

"I don't won't to talk about it, Shaniya. Just leave me alone!" Just before Shaniya walked away from the door she heard Skylar break down into sobbing. She started to beat on the door and then, suddenly, she was reminded how she liked being alone during embarrassing times.

"Whenever you're ready to talk, I'll be in my room." Shaniya spoke to the door as if it could talk back.

"Is she okay?" Brody asked. He had finally made it upstairs and away from the crowd downstairs. He felt awkward, watching Bryan get read by Kerry.

"Yeah, she'll be good. She's just a little embarrassed."

"Oh, okay. Did she tell you who she got into it with?"

"Nawl, she didn't tell me all that." Smoothly, Brody brushed up behind Shaniya.

"Well, I guess that leaves us all alone." He said, whispering into her ears, and then biting down on her earlobe.

"Brody, it's a house full of peoples." Gently, Brody popped Shaniya on her buttocks and then said, "That's what makes it fun." He joked as he followed Shaniya into the guess room.

"You so bad, I mean, really bad."

"Hell, it's so much chaos going on in this house, they won't even notice." Shaniya burst into laughter at Brody's joke then pound her fist into his tight muscles.

"Don't be talking about my family, buster." Brody broke into laughter, trying to dodge Shaniya's next punch.

"This family got more drama than the Kardashian."

"Shut up, stupid!" Again, Shaniya pound into Brody's chest. And before she could throw another, he grabbed her by the arm and pulled her in towards him. Without, warning he thrusted his tongue down her throat.

"Wait Brody, I need to go check on Skylar again." Brody jumped up from the bed and headed toward the room door. He was on Shaniya's tail, literally. When she reached the door, unlocked it, and tried to open it, he pushed it back shut. He then pressed her into the door, and she could feel his harden penis piercing the small of her back. It was hard, and it was very, very big.

"I got to go check on Skylar, you freak." Shaniya uttered trying to free herself from Brody's lock.

"She needs some me time, like I need some we time." Brody flashed his pearly white teeth and Shaniya couldn't resist. He was her favorite chocolate. He could go for Morris Chestnut little brother; body, smile, and all.

He started sucking on Shaniya's earlobe, drawing her hoop earring into his mouth along with the rest of it. When he stuck his thick, juicy tongue inside of her ear canal, fucking was a done deal. He had hit her spot.

"Turn around, Shaniya!" she loved when he demanded; he never asked. She turned around to face him, and before she made it all the way, he got down on his knees and started pulling down her denim, exposing her white lace panties.

"Damn!" he said at the site of Shaniya's beautiful view. He pulled her panties down. She lifted her legs up, one at a time, so he could get them over her white all-stars and completely off. He pushed her leg up and gently on his right shoulder and began to lick on her pussy lips with his thick tongue. She was trembling all over, halfway because she felt guilty about not checking on Skylar and halfway because she was feenin to see what was coming next. Shaniya loud moans echoed into Skylar room next door. All night she laid silent, in heat. Listening to Shaniya get her fire put out while she wondered why she was waiting for sex when everyone else wasn't.

"I can't believe I let you drag me out the house." Skylar searched through her purse for her lip gloss. Neatly, she painted her lips, and then checked for any flaws; sleepers, bookers, lose strains of hair, through the sun visor mirror.

"And I can't believe aunt Kerry lets us get the Benz. Anyway, you need to get out the house. Just sitting up in that house isn't going to help."

"Look at my damn face." Skylar glanced once more at her bruise face before closing the visor and jumping out the car.

"You honestly don't look that bad. I beat that face better than she ever could. Honey, you are slayed for the God's." Both Shaniya and Skylar flaunted their natural curves as they strutted into Lenox mall like they were worth millions. The shopping mall is sensory overload. The carefully styled images seduced consumers and wherever the eyes fail there was temptation; Victoria Secret, Bebe, Pandora, Apple, you name it. There is everything the girls want and very little they need. To move through the crowd meant Skylar getting closer to other people than she would usually want, but Shaniya insisted they do a little retail therapy.

"So, what's up with aunt? She got up snapping this morning. Ii could hear her all through the house." The girls took a scroll through bath and body works.

"Oh, aunt been snappy for a little while now. I don't know what's been up with her lately. It's like she's going through menopause or something."

"Nawl, she's too young for that." Shaniya picked up the coconut leaf candle and smelled it.

"Damn, I been looking all around for this scent. I wonder if they have the body lotion? Excuse me maim?" Shaniya waved her hand high at the nearest sale associates.

"Oh, I don't even believe this shit." Skylar mumbled.

"What?" Shaniya asked.

"That's Dontae's ex."

"The one you got into a fight with?" Shaniya squinch her eyes for a better look at Shanika.

"Yeah, that one." Skylar answered.

"Oh, well Merry Christmas to me." Shaniya strutted towards what seemed to be like the manager in full speed.

"Shaniya, don't do nothing stupid." Skylar whispered following closely behind Shaniya.

"Excuse me, are you the manager?" Shaniya asked the Caucasian lesbian.

"Yes, I am. Can I help you?"

"Yes, maybe you can because the sales associate over there sure couldn't. I had been waiting for her to help me for a minute and when I asked her did she forget about me, she just went off. I spend too much money in this store to be treated like I'm a nobody. Then she had the nerve to tell me to spend my money elsewhere then. My dollar is not the only dollar in the world!"

"Just calm down maim." Shaniya began to draw the attention of the customers, but Shanika had no idea what was going. She figured it was just another displeased customer complaining about the sale not being what it had exclaimed to be in the email ads.

"Oh, I'm calm but if yaw ever want my service again yaw better get rid of that ghetto ass Shanika." Shaniya stormed out the store and Skylar followed her. As soon as they were clear to laugh, they did. The two laughed like they were in a comedy club.

"You are stupid girl! I wouldn't have never thought to do that."

"That bitch won't be having a job." Shaniya said as she and Skylar stopped at the pretzel stand.

"Thanks, Shaniya."

"You know I got you baby. Now, let's get you a revenge outfit. It's time you show North Atlanta what the nerd been hiding them silly ass glasses and funny looking clothes." Both Skylar and Shaniya giggled their hearts away and the laughter felt good. Not once did Skylar think about the embarrassing night and not once did Shaniya think about hunting her.

5

Kerry morning is pretty much the same day after day: get up, start a load of laundry, a four-mile run around the local park, come back, and lift some light weights to tone her upper body, then a couple of sit-ups. She's no Teyanna Taylor but she could give Beyoncé post baby, Blue, a round for her money. Staying fit and keeping herself up was a must after the baby. She looked down on the women who let themselves go after getting married and having kids.

Just as Kerry throw the clothes in the dryer, her phone rang. She rushed to the living room, attempting to catch the phone before it stopped ringing. She had missed the call by a couple of seconds.

"Shit, I forgot I was supposed to meet Alexis today. Damn!" She murmured before rushing upstairs.

"What the hell can I slide on really quick?" Kerry pulled her back into a pony tail as she rushed into the bathroom for a quick shower. Ten minutes later, she threw on her best fitted distress jeans, a white fitted t-shirt, her favorite white air max 97 and headed into Atlanta congested traffic. Kerry blew her horn at people who cut her off or refuse to let her merge, losing her religion and becoming one of the heathens, changing lanes like a maniac. She had supposed to meet Alexis hours ago. She had prayed Alexis was late herself, so she wouldn't notice how late she was.

Alexis sat inside the cute little bed and breakfast, sipping on a cup of coffee, waiting on Kerry. She wanted to call her again to see what the holdup was, especially since Kerry had canceled on her three times in the last month. But she didn't want to harass her. Johnathan had been dead for a while now and it was time she moved on with her life, at least that's how Alexis felt others, like Bryan and Kerry thought. She'd sometimes feel like she was bothering them and that maybe they didn't want to be bothered with her no more since Johnathan was dead.

Alexis is staring out the window at the leaves blowing around the city. The sky is moody grey, and the wind is fall-time cool.

"Are you almost ready to order?" the waitress asked as she freshened Alexis coffee.

"Just give me a few more minutes, thanks." Finally, Alexis bit the bullet and called Kerry. On the second she picked up and answered, "I'm around the corner. I should be pulling up in a minute." Alexis was relief that Kerry didn't seem annoyed.

"Okay, did you want me to order for you?"

"No, you don't have to do that because I really don't know what I want but I'll be there shortly. This traffic was hell."

"Okay, cool." When Alexis spotted Kerry heading for her table as soon as she hung up the phone, her heart smiled.

"Chic, you were walking in already?" Alexis stood up to hug Kerry. Her scent was heavenly. Dove mixed with a hint of Rihanna's crush perfume.

"You smell fresh out the water." Alexis said before flopping back down into her seat.

"Yes, girl. I had to shower. You know I work out in the morning. But I'm so sorry I'm late. I honestly forgot about us meeting up today and when you called I hadn't even taken a shower yet." Alexis tooted her lips and crinkled her nose, "You little tramp. You been had me here waiting on you all this time and you done forgot that was even supposed to come today?"

"I know friend and I'm sorry. Thanks for waiting though. I really did need to get out the house." Kerry picks up the laminated menu in front of her and scans over it.

"Why, is life just too good for you, that you need a break?" Alexis joked.

"I think I already know what I want." Kerry slams the menu back down on the table.

"Actually, life is the complete opposite. I think I'm going through a crisis or something. Where is our waitress? She needs to come on, I'm hungry." Kerry waves her hand in the air, signaling she needed services.

"Honey, don't come up in here rushing this lady. She been waiting on your ass all day. Now, it's your turn to be patient." Without second thought, Kerry put her hand down and replied, "True."

"So, what are you going through that got you feeling like you're having a mid-life crisis?" Alexis asked before sipping more of her coffee.

"Well, for starters, I don't think my husband love me anymore, or he's lost interest or he's cheating or something. Hell, I don't know!" Alexis burst into laughter.

"You sound like one of them little white women off the TV whining about bullshit. Just looking for a reason to be unhappy."

"No, I'm serious!" Kerry explained.

'How are you serious and you don't even know why you're unhappy or what your husband has done to make you unhappy? That man loves you with every bone in his body. I honestly haven't seen any man love a woman so much. You're married, with a beautiful healthy baby, you don't have to work, and most importantly, you got your nieces back. They're even doing good. Hell, they could be out here running your ass crazy. Fucking with all kinds of low life little boys or smoking and popping them pills and shit these kids take now. But they're not. They in school, making good grades, you not getting no phone calls talking about they been caught stealing or none of that shit." Alexis had made her point, and everything she said made since, so why was Kerry so unhappy she wondered.

"Hey, ladies. Are you ready to order?" The thin red-hair Latina flashed her smile as she waited for the lady's order.

"Yes, I'm ready. I'll have your steak and gravy biscuit with a side of scrambled cheese eggs."

"And what would you like to drink?" Annabella asked Kerry.

"Umm… You can give me a glass of orange juice."

"Okay. And you miss?"

"I'll have your hash brown bowl; my meat will be sausage and I'll like a side of scrambled cheese eggs as well. And you can refill my coffee too, because that's gone." Alexi giggled a little at her large empty cup.

"Okay. I'll bring that right over."

"Thanks." The ladies said in unison.

"I don't like how you just down played my mid-life crisis." Kerry laughed at her own joke, but Alexis didn't join in on the laughter which was unusual for her. She never missed a chance to laugh.

"I'm not down playing baby. I just thought should give the view you couldn't see. You know, some of us are still out here looking for happily-ever-after." Kerry felt less than stupid as she looked into Alexis glistening eyes.

"You know, I thought I found my happily-ever-after with Johnathan and then *BOOM*, he's taken away from me. I know I supposed to be over him by now but sometimes I feel like he was the only hope I had at enjoying this life."

"Girl, don't be silly." Kerry could hear the crack in Alexis voice, so she tried to chime in with a little positivity.

"You and Johnathan would be happily married if he was here right now and you know that."

"I try to convince myself that but, it's questionable you know? I still think he and Shaniya had more going on then she led on, but she just didn't want to hurt my feelings with the truth." Kerry bluntly burst into laughter. She didn't care if it was rude, she wanted Alexis to hear herself. As she and Alexis took their meals from Annabella's hand, there was silence. They dug into their food and for about three long minutes nobody said anything.

"Listen, I'm not here to stroke your sorrow because believe it or not, I'm going through some shit but Alexis, really? You know damn well, Shaniya and Johnathan had nothing serious going on. He dated her mother for goodness sake. I know my niece and I know when they're lying, and she wasn't lying when I sat down and talked her about Johnathan. She told me what she told you. She was mad and wanted to make him mad, so she pretended to be his woman when you called.

"It's no way, Johnathan would even be able to look me in my eyes, walking around here with my niece on his arm knowing damn well he was with her mother. Girl, you are reaching now." Alexis took in what Kerry said and just like Kerry, she didn't see it that way.

"I guess you're right. I didn't look at it that way. I don't know, I just have so many questions that I never got to ask. You know?"

"Yeah, I feel you Alexis. I know that shit along hurts. But, look at it this way. Johnathan brought you to me before he left this world and ill forever be thankful for that." Kerry words made Alexis heart smile because Kerry was never the mushy type and she hardly ever said nice things. She was eighty percent bad ass and if she cried it was about her member of her family. No outsiders were ever allowed in her heart.

"See bitch, this is why we supposed to been met up. We need each other's more than we know." Alexis said before wiping her wet eyes with the napkin from the table.

"I know, I agree."

"Good. I'm glad you agree." Alexis blurted with a large Kool-Aid smile paste on her face.

"Oh, lord. I knew it was something."

"Yes, it's always something with me honey."

"Don't I know," Kerry responded before stuffing her mouth with food.

"I'm having a party for Johnathan. You know his birthday coming up and I just want to have a reason to celebrate with my close friends since I don't have much family."

"Chic, you have a party for everything."

"I know, but this is a legit reason. I'm celebrating my man, your friend's birthday."

"Okay, I'll call Bryan and see what he got going on and we'll make an entrance." Kerry shook her head, knowing she was going to regret committing to this party later.

"Good, no bagging out either Kerry." Alexis jumped up from the table.

"We'll be there." Kerry repeated.

"Okay, I'll be back. I got to use the restroom." Kerry dig through her purse for her phone. She hadn't spoke to Bryan all morning which was unusual. He'd usually been done called two or three times by now checking on her and the kids, who was with the hired part-time nanny. Bryan's mother, Claire.

"On the last ring, Bryan answered, "Hey baby. What's going on?"

"I was about to ask you the same thing. I haven't heard from you all day. Are you okay?"

"Oh, I just been tied up at the office. The firm is swamped. But I'm okay. I been meaning to call you and check on you and the kids. Are yaw okay?"

"Well, I'm out having brunch with Alexis but, yes everybody okay. What did you want to eat tonight?"

"Oh, I might be a little late tonight. I got to work on Chante case for her. She's here at the office."

"Chante?"
"Yes, baby. Chante. And it's nothing like that."

"Is she paying you for this service that's keeping you out late?" Kerry snapped.

"Baby the office is filling up. I got to go the meeting is about to start. I'll call you and kids later." Before Kerry could reject his dismal, she had heard the click. Her heart wanted to burst into salty tears, but she couldn't dare break down in public. She had heard everything Alexis told her earlier, but it didn't take away the feeling of being neglected and lonely. She wasn't used to this new Bryan. The Bryan she loved and knew catered to her every need. She felt like she was losing him or herself one.

As soon as Alexis resurfaced from the restroom, Kerry came up with an excuse to bounce.

"Girl, I got to get the kids from Claire. She said got to run the hospital for something. I got to go but I'll be at the party. Send me the details via text. We'll talk."

"Cool," Alexis said as she hugged Kerry.

"Oh, and don't worry about the bill I paid it already. My little way of saying sorry for keeping you so long." Kerry tried to joke her way out the restaurant because her heart was aching, and she felt like she would at any minute now.

"Oh, thank you baby. You're so sweet." Alexis blurted out to Kerry's back as she disappeared through the doors.

As soon as she was in the car and in moving traffic she broke into sobbing. Her life was falling apart only she couldn't put her finger on the exact problem. She loved Bryan and she knew he loved her too. She even trusted Bryan and knew deep down he wasn't cheating on her. She loved her nieces and she loved being their beckon of hope, and their stability but with all the peoples she had in her life including her baby boy, she felt like she had no one. When she arrived home, she sat in the car for hours listening to Pandora slow jams.

6

Kerry bounced baby Bryan on one hip and feed little Khloe with her free hand. The babies kept her busy. So, when she heard the loud taps on the door, she didn't bother rushing to see who was knocking.

"Who is it?" She blurted out as she slowly walked to the door.

"UPS!"

"UPS?" She questioned.

"Are you Kerry?"

"Yes." Kerry took the device and signed her name on the recommended line. Beautiful flowers had arrived by the courier, a slim man in a great hurry. He had thrust the gift into her arms with an unimpressive bow and walked away hurriedly, turning more sharply than courtesy allowed. The bouquet was all Kerry's favorites, mini-sunflowers, white daisies, and purple asters. It wasn't her birthday and she didn't have a new lover, she closed the front door and didn't bother searching for a card. She knew it couldn't be nobody but Bryan. And just like that, she wasn't mad at him anymore. The thought was just as beautiful as the flowers. She held the bouquet of flowers close to her nose and inhaled the lovely scent.

"Those are beautiful, who got you them?" Bryan startled Kerry. She quickly placed the flowers on the kitchen island.

"Who got them for me?" she asked.

"Yes, are those your flowers? Who got them for you?" Kerry couldn't be sure, but Bryan looked to be seriously, clueless about the flowers. She investigated the bouquet of flowers for a note and found it. Sure enough, Bryan didn't send Kerry the flowers. They were sent to Kerry from the girls with a note that read:

We thank you for all you do. Life without you, isn't a life worth living. Thank you, aunt Kerry, for being the mother and aunt we never had. Love your beloved nieces. (Shaniya and Skylar) Oh, and we're sure momma is so happy that you took us in. She's most likely looking down on us with a huge smile.

Kerry heart sank in. She could barely breath. Tears slowly dripped from her wet eyes as she read the note. It was the sweetest suggestion and she was thankful for the girl's warm words, but she was so disappointed that the flowers didn't come from Bryan.

"What is it, baby?" Bryan brushed up behind Kerry and instantly she inhaled his favorite cologne, Creed Aventus. His body felt hard in the right places and soft in the others. His soft touched sent chills up Kerry's spine as he gently squeezed her waist. He was still the finest man she had ever dated. In fact, his charming looks was part of the reason she took so long to take him seriously. Kerry wasn't all that into cute men. She always thought they were either gay or stuck on themselves, but Bryan was neither. His dark caramel complexion and muscular body was a perfect match, but he never acted holly than thou.

"There from the girls." She replied trying her best to hold back her tears. She really wanted to say, they should have been from you but instead she avoided the drama and said, "How sweet of them. They're always thinking of me. It's good to know somebody cares."

"Yes, that was very sweet of them." Kerry sarcasm went right over Bryan's head. He sipped from the coffee that Kerry had out for him and headed for the door.

"What time will you be in tonight?" She asked, stopping him at the door.

"It might be another long night. Don't wait up."

"Another long night, with your favorite cologne on. Okay, I definitely won't wait up." Bryan started to reply to

Kerry suspicion, but he didn't. He was running late. He didn't have the needed time to clear up the drama.

"Oh, hey aunt. I see you got the flowers?" Shaniya blurted out as she skipped over to the island where Kerry had a full breakfast spread waiting for them: Pancakes, bacon, cheese eggs, grapes, and strawberries.

"Oh, wow! I didn't know they were this beautiful." Skylar said as she trailed in behind Shaniya, pulling out her a chair at the island.

"Yes, girls. I got the flowers and the note was just beautiful. Thank you." Kerry walked over to the girls and gave them warm kiss on the cheeks, but they could feel something wasn't right with her. They knew something was bothering her and as soon as they could come up with a plan to ask her about it, they would.

"Hey, grandma Claire." Skylar and Shaniya sung in unison as soon as Bryan's mother walked through the door.

"Hey girls." Both baby Khloe and baby Bryan reached out to Claire. Little Bryan was practically jumping from Kerry's hand to Claire's.

"Go ahead and get some writing done. I got them." Mama Claire said as she lightened Kerry's burden. Taking over her motherly duties.

"Aunt, I can't wait to read your book. I know it's going to be bomb." Shaniya said to Kerry's back as she slowly dragged out the kitchen and to her home office. Which was a small room made into an office.

"So, what do you girls have planned for today?" Both Shaniya and Skylar looked at each other and burst out laughing.

"A little fundraising and a little of torturing." Shaniya answered.

"Shaniya, have you had time to spend with Khloe?"

"Yes, she was with me all night and, I'll be in the house all day tomorrow before I leave. I'm actually coming right back after this fundraiser I promised Skylar I would help her with."

"Okay. Just checking. Make sure, you slide her into your busy schedule."

"Oh, I am, grandma."

"Where is Brody? Have you ditched him for Skylar?"

"Something like that. He's over his mom's house, so we kind of ditched each other. I'll see him tomorrow too."

"Ooh okay. Well you girls have fun and try not to be too petty. It's tacky you know." Shaniya and Skylar burst back into laughing like a bunch of preteens.

"We won't be too petty, I promise." Skylar joked.

The wind howled as the students departed through the gates, hustling, and bustling down the school yard.

Friends say bye to each other with a hug or a playful punch while newcomers stood looking nervously for their rides. The seniors stood, tall and proud, confident born with experience.

"Is that Donta?" Shaniya said pointing over to the tall handsome muscular built ball player.

"Yelp, that's Mr. Hot shot." Skylar answered staring down the one boy to steal her heart.

"Damn, little sister you got taste." Seductively, Shaniya licked her lips as she and Skylar strutted over towards North Atlanta rowdy football team.

"It's game time little sister. Work his ass." Skylar was the kind of girl that cheerleaders loved to hate. She was a nerd with a hint of swag, but so beautiful that she was still in the drawing for most popular girl. Skylar had that movie star look, not overly tall and willowy, but more like an action star. Her muscle definition was perfect, and Shaniya taught her to walk with the confidence, like a decade older supermodel. She wasn't just flawless in her bone structure; her skin was smoother than a baby's bottom unlike most teens who suffered from ugly acne, and she exuded an intelligent sense of humor.

The football team watched on as she strutted her new exploited figure pass them. The makeover was to die for. The new blonde streaks, the fitted fashion nova jeans and clean lace body suit gave Skylar a fresh look. Her luminous kinky curls bounced as she strutted her thang to Brody's rented G-wagon. He was her rented boyfriend for the day, only he didn't have to show his face. Everyone assumed he was some college boy coming to scoop up Skylar from school. All Shaniya's idea, and it worked beautifully. Dontae couldn't take his eyes off Skylar. Her melanin was popping. Shaniya jumped back into her car, so she wouldn't blow Skylar cover and watched the scene from afar.

Shanika couldn't believe how good Skylar looked and neither could Dontae. He tried his hardest to distance himself from the boys and Shanika for two reasons; he didn't want Skylar to think he was talking to Shanika and secondly, he was embarrassed and didn't want to hear his boys clown him about being dissed by a nerd.

Bent over in the truck, Skylar flaunts her round her butt as she switched it side to side. She's talking about absolutely nothing to Brody, but Dontae doesn't know that. He was anxious to check Skylar as soon as she walked away from the truck.

"Skylar, don't you dare walk pass me and don't say nothing."

"Hey Dontae." Skylar said as she continued to walk to Shaniya's car.

"Come here, right quick." He demanded, trying to keep his voice at a medium tone so everyone couldn't hear what he was saying.

"I got to go, my sister waiting on me." Skylar soaked up the attention like a sponge on water. That'll teach

Dontae ass. Next time, he'll have her back more, she thought as he begged for her time.

"Man, just stop for a minute."

"What, Dontae?"

"What you got going on? Why you got niggas pulling up on you and shit, like I'm not right here?" Dontae was showing his feelings and Skylar loved every bit of it.

"I don't have time to play with you and your groupies, Dontae. You could have stopped that shit, but you sat back entertained. So just leave me alone and go back over there with your hood rats."

"Man, I told you I'm not with that girl. She just be tripping." Whatever, Dontae."

"Man, slow down. I'll take you home." Dontae chased behind Skylar like he wasn't the most popular boy in school. Roughly, he pulls on Skylar to slow her down.

"What?" Skylar snapped.

"I'll take you home. We need to talk." Skylar badly wanted to take Dontae up on his offer, but she knew it would ruin her plan. She investigated his light hazel eyes and concluded he wanted her bad. He brushed his waves, flashing his pearly white teeth, "You know you're just trying to make me jealous. I'm the only nigga you want. Who you think you fooling?" His charms and arrogance were his super power and worked on Skylar every time, but not this time. She wasn't folding.

"Whatever Dontae, call me when you're ready to be a man and not a little boy." Dontae unintentionally had a cheesy *I been chumped off* smile pasted on his face.

"Man, you are tripping girl." He said following close behind Skylar.

"Okay. Bye, Dontae." Skylar jumped into the car, and as soon as Shaniya pulled the car out the school yard, Skylar screamed to the top of her lungs.

"Did you see his face, oh my goodness!"

"Now, that's how you work a fuck boy, little sister!" Shaniya replied.

"Oh my God, thank you Shaniya. I could have never pulled that off without you." Skylar was on cloud nine, but she upgraded to clod ten when Dontae began to call her.

"Oh, this nigga is wearing his heart on his sleeves today." Shaniya said as Skylar flashed her phone to show Dontae popping up on the caller I.D.

"You got this girl, don't blow it. Let that nigga feel for a minute. He not going nowhere." Skylar obeyed Shaniya's instructions and stuffed her phone back into her purse.

"Girl, let's go eat somewhere." Skylar suggested.

"Look who got their swagger back? Okay, we can do that. Maybe, I'll even order a drink and let you sip."

Shaniya flashed her dimples, then responded, "Fine by me."

"Oh, I'm loving this new Skylar. Good Job!"

7

It seemed like just yesterday Shaniya was leaving home for college. Two years later and she still wasn't used to the good byes. Skylar was in tears, baby Khloe wouldn't let go of Shaniya's leg until she bribed her with candy, Bryan was out at work and Kerry was pissed to the third degree. She washed dishes with such anger that everyone could hear the plates clink over the kid's noisy game of hiding seek. She had recently called Bryan to set him straight for missing dinner with the family and missing Shaniya leave and everyone in the house had to suffer the aftermath.

As chaotic as the house was, Shaniya hated leaving home. College was nothing like being home. But Shaniya knew that she wasn't just living for her now. She had a little life that depended on her. And there was no way she could disappoint Khloe. She wanted to be a mother her daughter could be proud of.

"Bye everybody. I love yaw." Shaniya said for the third time before shutting the door behind her. Brody patiently waited for Shaniya by the car. As she slowly approached him he noticed the sparkle in her eyes.

"What's wrong? Why you look like you about to cry?" Shaniya pouted like a toddler as she handed over her bags to Brody.

"Because, I don't want to go." Shaniya whined.

"Get in the car crybaby." Brody joked. Shaniya plopped down into the car with her hands folded on her full breast, with her glossed plumped lips tooted out. Not even ten minutes into the ride, Shaniya was out cold. The rain dripping on the windshield was better than Nyquil. Future, *HNDRXX* album entertained Brody as he cruised down the road. Before he could notice how tired he was, he'd reached his exit. Five minutes away from campus, Brody noticed a car tailing him weaving dangerously in and out of traffic.

Half blinded by the glare of headlights, he couldn't make out the car or who was possibly in it but he knew the car had been following them through three red lights and two stop signs. He looked over at Shaniya and initially, he wanted to wake her, but he thought about how dramatic she would act and that wouldn't help their situation at the moment, so he didn't.

Onslaught of bullet sized rain drops thundered onto the windshield, wipers frantically moving over the never-ending sheet of water, blurring the street. If Brody wasn't so familiar with the streets he and Shaniya would probably be throwed over in a ditch somewhere. The unmarked car chased his red smudge tail lights. His back end skidded out wildly around corners, their tires squealed, engine pushed to the limit, over 75 km/ph through red lights, and stop signs and not once did Shaniya wake up. She was sort of used to Brody driving like a bat out of hell, so his speedy driving wasn't dramatic enough to scare her awake. Brody adrenaline was pumping, he could barely keep his nerves together.

"Who the fuck is this?" He murmured with his eyes fixated on the glare in the review mirror. Three more risky turns and Brody finally shook the car. He quickly pulled into the campus parking lot, closer to the security booth than his room.

"Come on Shaniya. Get up, we here!" He blurted out.

"Why are you yelling?" Shaniya woke up stretching for the stars and just as she was about to pull the sun visor down to check for cold in her eyes, Brody screamed out, "We don't have time for all that. Let's go Shaniya, now!"

"Why are you acting like a crack patient. Chill out, man. Damn!" Brody grabbed Shaniya's bag from the back seat and slammed the door behind him.

"Okay, you stay your ass in the car, he blurted out before walking off. Quickly, Shaniya jumped out the car. The doors locked automatically behind her.

"Wait up, Brody. Damn!" Swiftly, she walked Brody.

"You must have to use the restroom?" She yelled out to his back.

"Yeah, and you taking all fucking day and shit!" he lied.

"I told your butt not to eat all them damn tacos in the first place. Being all greedy and shit."

"And why you bring me to your room?" Short of breath, Shaniya struggled to keep up with Brody's pace.

"You're staying with me tonight."

"You don't think you should have maybe asked me this first?"

"No, Shaniya. Damn! Just bring your ass on." Obeying, Shaniya just followed behind Brody closely. She was too sleepy to argue with him. As soon as they reached the room Shaniya jumped right into Brody's bed. She didn't even take notice to his paranoia. He paced the room like a mad man. He looked out the window every five seconds. After two hours, he had finally concluded they were safe and he jumped into bed with Shaniya.

"Sha-ni-yah!!!" Skylar piercing voice cut through the air like lighting cut through the sky, causing Shaniya to stop instantly. She turned back with tears streaming down her face, and her heart fell into her stomach. Brad's goons had caught Skylar. Indecision pulsed through Shaniya as her eyes quickly scanned her surroundings. There were no police in sight, not a stranger nearby. No nosey women, no loud kids, and definitely no heroic men. A completely ghost town. Shaniya ran towards Skylar but before she could reach her, Skylar was forced in the back of the black Cadillac truck.

"Shaniya!" Skylar screamed.

"Skylar!" yelled back, crying as she watched the vehicle begin to drive away. Don't take her, take me. Please!" A mob of men surrounded her and stood to her feet in terror. They grabbed at her body. Apart of Brad sick game of torture, they floundered her and snatched at the thin fabric of her clothes. She tried to fight through the maze of spiteful men, but they overpowered her. Shaniya was tossed back and forth, from man to man, as they cruelly played with her. They pushed her so hard that she fell to the ground as she seeped, her face falling hopelessly in her hands. Finally, Brad said, "Leave her alone. I got her from here."

"No!... No! Please Brad, don't kill me."

Brody turned to his side and gently, awakened her out of her horrific dream.

"Shaniya... Baby, Shaniya, wake up. It's just a dream," he said as he brushed the hair out of her face and sat beside her on the bed. Shaniya looked around the dorm room and shook her head, bringing herself back to reality. She was safe and there was no Brad around.

God please watch over my family, she silently prayed as she put her hands over her face and groaned in frustration. Shaniya heart raced, and the horror she felt was as fresh as Public's fruits. She could barely tell the different from reality and her horrific dream. She sat up straight and breathed deeply as she closed her eyes. Her hands went to her clammy face as she shook her head.

"It was just a dream, Shaniya. It was just a dream." She repeated in a sincere whisper as she wiped the tear that slid down her face.

"What was the dream about, who is Brad, Shaniya?" Brody asked with a lost expression on his face. Shaniya shook her head in dismissal and waved her hand.

"Nothing. It not something I can talk about with you. Trust me, it's for your own good."

"Let me be the judge of that, Shaniya."

"Just let it go, Brody! Damn." Shaniya slid back down into bed, hoping she could dodge the conversation by drifting back to sleep.

"When you ready to talk, I'm ready to listen." Brody said before sliding back into the covers with Shaniya.

8

When Shaniya heard the band, it was like liquid adrenaline being injected right into her blood stream – her nerves instantly disappeared, and her heart tingled as she started to move her body rhythmic to the drums.

She'd never had a dance class, but she and her early child hood friends had danced to music in the neighborhood, competing in the friendly way girls do to "up" one another. Now, the co-captain of the majorette team, she was a well-oiled machine in the stands. She didn't dance to show off, to make the boys watch - but they did. Her body was perfection in the shimmery form fitting custom.

Dancing was therapeutic for Shaniya. It was as if it were the only way her body truly knew how to speak to her troubling soul. She felt free with every eight count she threw. At the games her personality, and her sensuality shined like blood diamonds. Brody watched Shaniya for a quick minute, dance with the band entertaining the stadium, and then his attention went back to the groupie that giggled at his every word. She was thicker than a snicker, bright like the stadium lights with bold red freckles in her face. Watching with her hawk eye, Shaniya blood began to boil. As she turned her attention towards Brody, she caught him standing there, nervous, trying to hide in the crowd of basketball players.

He dropped his eyes momentarily before looking up at Shaniya, his head tilted to one side and then Shaniya read his lips tell the flirt Juicy, "Yo, bag back. You are invading a nigga space. You know damn well my girl watching a nigga like a hawk." Brody probably would have talked his way out the dog house had he not been joking when he told juicy to bag off. To Shaniya, he enjoyed the attention. Soaking it up like water into a flower. Girls was Brody weak spot. Girls, was the reason Brody was in the stands and not on the field with his team. He had been accused of sexual harassment and was currently benched until the investigation was over.

As soon as the band was dismissed by the director, Shaniya strutted over towards Brody and his boys. Everybody knew what was about to go down, including Juicy. Slowly, Juicy attempted to fade away through the crowd but Shaniya stopped her in her tracks with her harsh words.

"Yeah, as soon as you turn on the lights the hoes get to scattering like roaches. Don't go nowhere no hoe!"

"First of all, who are you calling a hoe?" Juicy snapped, rolling her store bought emerald eyes.

"Bitch, I'm talking to you! Fuck you mean?" Swiftly, Shaniya charged towards Juicy, but she didn't get to pound her face in like she wanted to because Brody quickly pulled her back before she could reach Juicy personal space.

"Man, chill out with that." Brody said attempting to pull Shaniya away from the crowd and Juicy.

"Chill out with that?" And just like that, Shaniya was ready to gun for Brody again.

"How fucking dare, you tell me to chill out when you're the one out here entertaining these hoes and shit!"

"I wasn't fucking entertaining no damn body! Chill with that fucking drama shit bruh for real."

"You always trying to make it seem like it's me with the drama when you're the fucking one who always igg the shit on Brody. If your ass was to keep your fucking attention on the game and not these hoes, you'll be out there on the field bettering your chance to be draft. But naw, you still hooked on hoes like kids in a candy store!" Shaniya voice echoed over the loud clatter in the stadium. Everybody's attention was on her and Brody. Brody beyond embarrassed, his boys was watching, some groupies he had his eyes on, and some teachers he had mad respect for. He attempted to just stay quiet, hoping his silence would make Shaniya drop it, but she didn't. She kept right on, and on, and on until he exploded.

"That's why a nigga be out here in these streets doing what he does because you run a nigga crazy with all your fucking drama. Shit! I been dropped the shit and you still fucking mouthing off. And soon as a nigga return the favor, you'll think I'm wrong." Shaniya wanted to cry as rage filled her belly. She felt her ears getting hot. She glared at him then spat out, "WHO THE FUCK YOU TALKING TO?" He sneered at her then laughed only adding fuel to her wrath.

"Oh, you think this shit is funny?" She snapped, mushing her index finger into his forehead. He scowled at me with hatred in his cruel dull eyes.

"Keep fucking pushing me Shaniya. I'm going to hurt your fucking feelings out here?" he said calmly but their heated quarrel continued. It was a war of words and a contest of who can hurt the other one worse. Both at each other throats like savage hungry dogs fighting over red meat.

Once Shaniya made her point that she was irreplaceable, she walked off on Brody. He stood stupidly outside the stadium, refusing to chase after her. She had decided to catch an Uber back to her dorm. Shaniya could barely hold back her tears as she slowly walked to her room. She was in no rush, since she wanted to calm once she reached her room. The last thing she needed was Amber asking her what was wrong. So, she took her time walking to the room, taking in the cool-late fall breeze and fresh air.

I bet you I'm not talking to his ass all week, watch this. She thought to herself before the heavy footsteps startled her. She checked her surroundings; left, right, then behind her but there wasn't a person in sight. Maybe she was just hearing things, she concluded before she continued her therapeutic walk.

Always got hoes in his face. I'm going to show his ass. When I start acting like him, he going to think I'm wrong. Again, Shaniya hear the footsteps. This time they seem closer. Just as she's about to turn around to check if someone's behind her, she notices the shadow on the concrete. Indeed, it was someone behind her; tall, built with some sort of weapon in their hand. Phone already in her hand, Shaniya quickly dialed Brody's number, but he didn't answer. She smoothly hung him up but continued to talk as if she had reached him.

"Hey, I'm outside, where are you?" She said loudly, while increasing her speed.

"Well, you can come on outside. I'm like right here." Shaniya noticed her little trick wasn't working. The stranger who was clearly a man, continued to follow her. As she sped up, so did he. At this point, it was no secret that he was following her. *I would have on heels*; As she attempted to kick them off her heart beats faster and the adrenaline demanded she run, right now, no delay. But unless she gets them off she can't. She wished to God they were sensible but were three inches high. Then the cold, wet near-winter concrete kissed her soul the moment her flat feet hit the ground. Quickly, she darted away into the darkness, running for the yellow light of the building ahead. Her feet slipped, and she almost tumbled over, more times than she can afford. Then she hears the creep keys rattling along with coins in his pocket, he's picked up his speed now and running closely down the narrow path behind Shaniya.

She prayed for a drunk crowd of frat boys to appear from one of the buildings, they often did at nighttime. There are now two pursuers; huge, fast, hyped up, likely horny or mentally ill. Shaniya couldn't figure out when the second joined the race, but she was sure that there was two of them chasing her. Before she knew it, she'd decided to scream.

"Help me! Help me, please!" Her voice rented the air and the desperation in it shook her own nerves. She sounded like someone in a movie, only being chased was nothing like the movies. The stars looked heroic, sexy and in command of the situation. Reality was far removed from that pretty version of running to save your life. Her feet slipped outwards on the wet autumn leaves as she rounded the corner, the cold night air shocking her throat and lungs as she inhaled deeper and faster.

Her heart beats frantically, but suddenly she remembered a short cut to her room. One up on the creeps, she knew the campus better than them. One quick turn and Shaniya opened the back door to a building that didn't seem to have any door. She leans against the wall to catch her breath. She was sure they didn't see where she had disappeared to. She waited a minute before climbing the steps, just to see if they had caught on to her running inside the building. Twenty seconds later, there was no movement. She peeked outside the door and she saw no one. Quickly, she skipped over to the building that led her to her dorm room.

9

Brody barely got a foot in the door before Shaniya began to call him names, reminding him that she was still very much pissed at him for flirting with the groupie at the game, talking to her with so much disrespect, and mostly for not taking her home. Before she could finish her insult, "You bastard, you couldn't even take me..." his phone rings again.

"Are you serious, right now?" Shaniya blurted out to Brody as he reached into his pocket to grab his IPhone.

"It's my momma, crazy ass girl." Brody answered the phone with abruptness, "Can I call you back?" He snaps, "Who you talking to like that?" Brody mother Kim snapped back.

"I'm sorry momma. Me and Shaniya was having intense argument and I didn't won't you to hear that."

"Is everything okay?" Kim asked.

"Yeah, everything fine. I'm going to call you back momma." Brody feels bad for rushing his mother off the phone, since he's never available when she wants to talk. So, he readjusts his tone and the direction of the conversation, "Did you get some tickets today from the store?"

"Yes, I haven't even scratched them off yet. I'm feeling lucky though. When I hit big, I got you." Brody giggled a little and then, he gets quiet. Kim know he's annoyed and wants to hang up, so she wraps the conversation up.

"Well, let me scratch these tickets off baby. I'll talk to you later. Make sure you and Shaniya talk it over with each other feelings in mind."

"Yeah, that's what I'm trying to get her to understand now." Shaniya looked over at Brody, rolled her eyes, and blurted, "Don't be over there lying to your momma Brody because you know this is all your fault."

"Girl, be quiet. I'm not talking about you started nothing. Momma, I'm call you back."

"Okay, baby." Quickly, Brody pocket his phone, and then swiftly charged towards Shaniya. She snatched back from his reach and ran towards the door, but he was on her tail.

"I done told you about your damn mouth." Aggressively, Brody hemmed Shaniya up against the door.

"You let me go home by myself, what kind of man…" Before Shaniya could finish her sentence, Brody thrust his tongue down her throat. He wasn't the best kisser in the world, but his cockiness turned Shaniya completely on. She craved him; she straddled her legs around his waist as he buried his tongue deeper into mouth. He could have sucked both her lips clear off and she wouldn't have cared. Shaniya loved how powerful Brody was. He handled her like a light weight. She could feel his dick, hardened, in between her legs. She couldn't wait to feel him deep inside of her. She would just have to tell him about being chased later.

He pulled her Savannah state sweatshirt off over her head. Then removed her bra that was covering her small but perky breast. Shaniya derived much pleasure from having Brody suck all over them. Her nipples could have cut sheetrock. She took the tip of her tongue and licked inside his ear, then she bit down gentle on his earlobe. It was Brody soft spot. Brody let Shaniya down just long enough to finish taking off both his and her clothes, which he did with a quickness. Within the next few minutes, her vagina was leaking juices.

He picked her back up against the wall, with sweat cascading down both their bodies, and Shaniya could feel the head of his dick rubbing up against her baby-fine pussy hairs. His tone body felt so good up against her small frame.

"Awww, daddy." She moaned as soon as his huge dick invaded her pussy walls, pushing deep inside of her.

Shaniya didn't give it to Brody often, so she still felt paralyzed at his first strokes. A man with a big dick usually gives you that shock factor. Brody always had to stroke Shaniya a couple of times before she could maneuver her pelvic muscles on it. Shaniya started kissing him deeply and palmed the back of his head like a basketball. His dick was always the bomb. They fucked for a quick twenty minutes, and then he came. Shaniya could feel his hot cum shoot up inside her and instantly she thought about her aunt Kerry words, *don't your ass get pregnant again. You need to graduate and get a job first*.

    It was a warm windy fall day: perfect for a day at the fair. After they quickie, Shaniya and Brody decided to go out for some alone time together. Shaniya roommate Amber had come back for studying and they didn't won't to disturb her.

    The sky was dotted with a few candy-floss clouds. Making the long wait not seem so long. The entrance could be seen in the distance and the long lines edged forward slowly. Customers were becoming increasingly excited and impatient as they took a few steps forward every so often. Faint music could be heard from beyond the tall gates with the occasional happy screams suddenly piercing the air. The closer they got to the entrance, the massive structures of the rides could be seen: a rollercoaster, a big wheel, a long slide, and bumper cars.

"Man, I haven't been to the fair in years. I got to take Khloe." Shaniya said as she swayed side-to-side in Brody's arms; her back against his chest.

"Yeah, she'll love this shit. Me and my brothers couldn't get enough of it."

I know right. Me and Skylar couldn't go as much as we wanted to either. My momma would be like, *honey money doesn't grow on trees. One time is enough."* Brody gently kissed Shaniya on her forehead and said, "I know you must miss her so much."

"You have no idea. I mean, it's like I see her every time I look into Khloe's eyes. She looks just like my mother pictures. She would have loved Khloe to pieces, but I probably wouldn't have Khloe because she wouldn't play that shit. She watched over like a hawk."

"That's how you got to be on baby Khloe." Before Shaniya could respond to Brody, she turned to face the familiar face in line behind her; too slow to be normal. When she spoke her voice trailed slowly, like her words were unwilling to take flight.

"Oh, I don't even believe this shit." She mumbled. There is a sadness in her eyes, the brown too glossy.

"What? What you see?" Shaniya never broke her stare, nor did she answer Brody. Swiftly she walked off. Heading full speed towards her target.

"It was you following me last night wasn't it?" Aggressively, Shaniya mushed her index finger into Chance temple. He saw her wrath coming the moment their eyes locked, so he didn't trip. He just kept his calm.

"Shaniya, come on. You are tripping, man. You got peoples looking at us all crazy and shit." Brody said as he attempted to pull Shaniya away from Chance.

"Answer me, Chance! Was it you following me last night? What the fuck are you even doing here in the first place?" All eyes fixated on Shaniya as she threw her tantrum so carelessly in front of everyone.

"Then you here with a bitch!" The terrified Asian lady eyes widen. She didn't know what was going on.

"So, what, you've started a whole fucking family now?" Brody badly wanted to walk off on Shaniya but there was something holding back. He was beyond embarrassed.

"Shaniya, chill out!" He blurted pulling her away from Chance.

"Don't you tell me to fucking chill! Someone followed me last night to my room Like literally chased me down, and I want to know if it was you Chance?" Shaniya snatched away from Brody again and turned back around to face Chance.

"What a fucking coincidence that I see you today?" Chance silence made Shaniya look like a complete fool. He didn't utter a word. He and the Asian woman beside him just stood still with confusion purposely pasted onto their face.

"If you don't bring your ass on, I'm about to leave you. The police coming and shit! You're going to get a nigga kicked out of school." Shaniya heard Brody, but she wasn't leaving to she blurted, "Why you are following me and shit; how about you come and see your fucking daughter. You know, your first child. Why you done ran off to build a whole new family. You fucking coward ass nigga." Shaniya knew instantly from the look in Chance eyes that her words had hit their mark. Shaniya knew Chance was everything but a *coward ass nigga* but she also knew them words would burn his soul, along with breaking the news that baby Khloe was indeed his.

She continued with the rage, throwing her words like darts. Words flew from her mouth that she never thought she'd even think, let alone say aloud in public. She shoved him, mushed him, and even punched her fist into his broad muscular chest a couple of times but he still tried his best to hide his emotion. Even though, he wasn't fooling her. Shaniya knew it wouldn't be the last she'd hear from Chance. She had stumped his pride; whatever relationship they had were shattered into glassy shards. Nothing would ever be the same again.

Shaniya words caught Brody off guard. *His daughter*, he thought before staring Chance down. Sure enough, Khloe was his twin. Her complexion glowed like her mothers with a Hershey topping but her hair was silk and surly. Now, it all made sense to Brody, baby Khloe was mixed with Puerto Rican. Baby Khloe was a split image of her grandmother Khloe and her father Chance.

"This Khloe daddy?" Brody questioned with an attitude.

"Yes, that's his sorry ass. How fucking dare, you man? How dare you?" Shaniya repeated as Brody pulled her away from the scene.

10

For as long as Skylar could remember, she had always been shy. Shy in school. Shy around friends. Shy about relationships with boys. She was definitely shy when it came down to her to talk to Kerry about her period and sex. She couldn't figure out if it was something deep-rooted inside of her from her early childhood experience or whether it was something that was just meant to be.

Skylar lived in her own little world by the time she reached high school. She is a paid intern for a nonprofit organization. She selected the job because she didn't want to deal with too many peoples on the daily basis. As the project coordinator, she only had to answer to one person, whom she'd grown very close to. And she was thankful for that. Her daily routine consisted of going to school, then to work, and occasionally, stopping at the library on the way home. Then retiring to her cozy but cramped bedroom. Only to repeat the same exact steps the next day. There was nothing Kerry or Shaniya could do to break her out of her shell. Sometimes, her personality would come out, but it was never long before she went back to the little timid shy good girl. At least, that's until she met Dontae. He had changed her life over the course of the months, and suddenly, she was this girl no one recognized.

For last couple of days, she had been torturing Dontae. Her silence was killing him softly. She wouldn't answer any of his calls, she sent every gift he had given her back; flowers, edible arrangement, and the promise ring. And finally, three weeks later, she was ready to put end to the torture.

Keeping to routine, Shaniya decided to study at the library before going home. As usual, it was empty. The library was so dead, the librarian was nodding on and off to sleep at her desk. She was so tired, she didn't even hear when Dontae walked into the library. He walked in with Jay-z confidence, looking like he could be some kin to Omari Hardwick. Mocha complexion, bow-legs, and a clean fade. It was no secret, Dontae didn't blend with the library scenery. Draped in Gucci and Jordan's, he only came to disturb the peace. Skylar peace that is. He knew her schedule like the back of his hand, and he was tired of being avoided so he pulled up on her. Only he didn't speak.

He looked over at Skylar and she looked up at him. His eyes seemed to have passion burning inside of them. He was so happy to see her, and she was happy to see him, only she didn't portray it right off. She sat there at a table across the aisle from where he was standing at a book case flipping through some pages, as if he was really interested in anything in the book. Skylar could feel her panties becoming damp from growing desire to feel him inside her. She crossed her legs and moved them back and forth, creating a light friction against her vagina and making her desire even more intense. Skylar didn't even realize she was sucking on the eraser of her pencil as stared at him, until she felt him staring back. She moved her eyes up from where they had locked on the bulge of his pants to his face, and for what seemed like an endless moment, their eyes met again.

Dontae broke the stare and smiled at her. It was then that Skylar noticed he had the softest-looking lips. She yearned to draw the bottom one into her mouth to suck on it. She was tired of being safe, and she was ready to give herself away, to Dontae. She looked back down at the biology book she was studying for a brief moment, waiting for him to make his move because she knew without a doubt he was only there to see her.

When she looked back up, Dontae was gone. Skylar panicked, scanning the library quickly, until she noticed him getting going to the supply room in the back of the library. He looked at her and smiled as he closed the door behind him. Something within her exploded, and she knew what had to be done. She quickly jumped up from the table, leaving her books, coat, and purse and ran down the aisle to the back of the library. As soon as she opened the door to the room, he was standing right by the door. She bumped into right into his chest and could feel her heart pounding up against his as he looked deep into her eyes, up close and personal for the first time in weeks.

He opened his mouth to say something, probably to ask her why she been avoiding him, but she put her finger over his lips. She was for the first time in her life, courageous. She didn't have sweaty palms and her knees wasn't trembling like they usually would do when she was close to boys. Skylar smiled at Dontae, locked the door, and took him by the hand, and pulled him deeper into the room.

"What are you doing?" Donate asked with a million-dollar grin on his face.

"I thought I told you not to talk." Skylar was without a doubt a beautiful girl. And now that she knew it, she was even more sexier. Their clothes came off quickly, both of them ripping at the other's until they were completely naked in the dimly lit room. She took one of her fingers and rubbed it against her clit, taking it putting it into her his mouth. He had watched enough explicit movies to know how it was done. All she had to do now was put the moves the test.

Dontae savored her juice off her finger. Then they began to kiss, both savoring her sweetness at the same time. He pushed her back on the crowded table so that her head was hanging halfway over the rear and her nipples were protruding upward into the air. He suckled on them one at a time, not only taking her dark pearls into his mouth but licking the entire breast, starting at the base of each one with the tip of his tongue and making light, globular strokes until he reached the hardened prize. Skylar was in ecstasy. So many nights had been spent alone rubbing her nipples between her fingers, and now her first love was devouring them just like she had yearned for all that time. Dontae took them both up one in each hand, pushing them together and then sweeping both nipples into his mouth at the same time.

Her moans were out of control, so Dontae covered her mouth with his hand because he knew she get louder just as soon as he penetrated her. Dontae and Skylar could have made a porn and it would have sold for millions. They made love and had sex all at the same time. Skylar shocked herself, even she couldn't believe her moves. She simply let her hormones guide her. When they were all done, the two went to the waffle house for food before Dontae dropped Skylar off at home. The night to her was perfect, nothing like the romance books she read; flowers, candy, music, and poems but perfect.

11

Kerry had to force herself out the house. After Bryan fleeked on her, she was in no mood to party, but she was obligatory to attend Alexus party for Johnathan. She had given her word she would be there. Bryan assured Kerry it was work but she couldn't help but think it was more of Chante than work that was holding him up. Since Chante reappeared in Bryan's life he hadn't been the same and Kerry was starting to see him less and less. She'd never been the jealous type, but she was slowly starting to get in her feelings about her husband close relationship with his hot friend.

Kerry assumed getting out the house for a while would help her take her mind off Bryan, but it didn't. So, she set in the corner of the room throwing back shots of Tequila hoping getting drunk would do the trick. As she watched Alexus and her guess dance their life away, the room slowly started to spin, and the quantity of people had doubled.

"Come on, get up and dance with me!" Alexus shouted across the room at Kerry.

"I know you didn't come here to just watch the fun." Alexus shouted over the loud music as the hardwood floors beneath her four-inch pumps racketed from her intensive twerking. The shiny hardwood had seen more dancing shoes than a ballroom. Since Jonathan's death, Alexus had turned her house into the party shack. The company of others helped her numb her pain and neglect her memories of Johnathan.

"Awe, that's my shit!" Kerry yelled out with her hand waving in the air as soon as the beat to Juvenile, *'Back that ass up'* came on. The music escaped from every window and door. All of Kerry and Johnathan closes friends ran to the dance floor. It was where they twirked, everyone with everyone. The party was lit like Alexus personality.

After grinding in the chair like a horny Jamaican for half the song, Kerry finally decided to get up and dance. She felt as steady as a leaf in a storm, "Oh shit," she mumbled before losong her balance. Kerry eyes widen in shock, and she was falling to the floor. A floor that would most likely bruise her if she continued to fall at the rushed speed. The wind from the fan left of her pushed against her face, she closed her eyes, waiting for the inevitable.

Just as she assumed, she'd hurt her knees, hands and elbow. Her knees were reddened, and her elbows were aching, and she couldn't move. She just laid flat on the floor watching the room spin like a turntable. Alexus laughed until she couldn't anymore. She had never saw Kerry so drunk.

Hurriedly, Johnathan old friend Derrick rushed over to Kerry's rescue.

"Are you okay?" Kerry glanced up at Derrick and giggled. All night she had been watching Derrick and now, finally when she was on the floor, drunk with her knees scraped, she gets his attention.

"Yeah, I'm good. I might have to lay here for a minute though." She joked as she gawked at Derrick like he was a live Picasso.

"Come on, let me help you help you." *Damn he fine*, Kerry thought as Derrick pulled her up from the floor by one hand. *And he tall to,* Kerry thought as she secretly sized up the gentlemen of the night. He stood six-foot-two, his complexion was in the mix, not too dark or too light but café au lait. He had enough muscles to lend three other brothas some and still be sexy as hell. His cinematic smile was contagious, as he smiled at Kerry she blushed back.

"Come on, I need you to help me with something." Kerry demanded as she guided Derrick to the guess bedroom. "Where are you taking me?" Derrick stopped in his tracks, refusing to go into the bedroom.

"Come on," Kerry commanded. "I need you to help me with something." Aggressively, Kerry grabbed Derrick by the hand and led deep into the bedroom and the guess room bathroom.

"What is it, you need help with Miss?" Kerry giggled some more and then Derrick followed her suit. Her goofiness was sort of turning him on.

"Don't worry, I'm not going to bit you." Kerry joked before she let down the straps of her black sequin dress. Derrick looked at her, dumbfounded. He didn't know what Kerry was doing.

"I need help unbuckling this damn girdle, can you help me?" Kerry said before bursting into laughter again.

"And hurry please before you witness me peeing on myself." Nervously, Derrick struggled to unbuckle Kerry's black girdle. He could barely stay focus, distracted by Kerry's beauty. His hormones had easily taken the best of him and his slowly his dick had arisen.

"Hurry, hurry! I'm going to pee." Kerry bounced up and down like a toddler in a tight.

"I'm sorry, I'm trying, it's not unlatching."

"Here, unbuckled it from here then," Kerry plopped one foot up on the tub, and then guided Derrick's hand down the center of her vagina. There were three rows of buckles that needed to unlatch for her freedom. Hesitantly, Derrick fondle with the buckles. The thickness of Kerry's pussy lips had hardened his dick more, but Kerry paid no attention, she just wanted freedom from the waist cinching girdle.

"If you don't hurry up, I'm going to piss all over you." Kerry words had motivated Derrick and quickly he had freed her. Speedily, she plopped down on the toilet and began peeing. The sober Kerry would have never, but the drunk Kerry didn't care a lit that Derrick was standing there. She had to go and a man watching wasn't going to stop her. Even if he was a stranger.

"Wait... Where you going? Don't you want to button me back up?" Kerry joked.

"No, silly girl. Just slide your dress over the damn thing. You might have to pee again." Derrick replied on his way out the door. Quickly, Kerry jumped up from the toilet, flushed it and washed her hands.

"Wait a second." She demanded as she followed behind Derrick.

"What is it now? Do you need your shoes taken off?" He kidded.

"Well, actually I do. It makes me dizzy to look down." Kerry responded while blushing.

"Come on here." Smoothly, Derrick scooped Kerry up off her feet. Her jumped hormones jumped like a jack rabbit. He smelled heavenly. Tightly, she wrapped her arms around his tight body as he toted her over to the bed. Gently, he laid her down and then slid her shoes off.

"No, need to put back on your dress. You've hit your limit for tonight. Just lay down and pray the pain isn't to harsh to you in the morning." Kerry boldly slid her hands under Derrick's black muscle tee and rubbed his perfect chest.

"Stop it, woman." He demanded.

"Why? Your friend down below, doesn't want me to." Kerry replied as she slowly slid her hand down Derrick's hard chest to his hardened dick. Her touch was magical, and his dick jumped. He wanted her more than a robber wanted money, but he knew better.

"How often do you drink?" he asked.

"I never drink?" she replied. "Exactly," Derrick quickly snatched Kerry's hand from his pants

"What?" she snapped.

"You are drunk baby, and you'll only regret this in the morning." He said.

"Assuming I remember it." Kerry replied.

"Oh, you'll remember it. Trust me."

"So, you say." Kerry snapped before pulling Derrick back into her personal space for a kiss. Their tongues locked and wrestled each other's for minutes. It was the sloppiest kiss Derrick ever had and he loved it, but he just wasn't about to take advantage of Kerry, not when he knew she was so vulnerable. He pulled back from her, attempting to walk off again.

"Okay, I want beg, but damn that kiss was good." Kerry joked. Derrick turned around and asked, "Oh, you liked that?"

"Yelp." Kerry quickly replied. "Well, you love this." Derrick speedily walked back over to Kerry and slid her to the end of the bed by her legs. He must've had the munchies because he wasted no time eating her pussy. He spread her thick pussy lips open with his long fingers and then gave her one hell of a tongue-lashing with his thick, juicy tongue. He was starved for her, he didn't come for air. Kerry rubbed his bald head deep in between her cum drenched thighs and rubbed it around, he looked like a glazed doughnut between her legs. She grabbed the back of his head and pushed his tonged deep into her pussy as if she was trying to brand his facial features into her vaginal lips. He ate on Kerry until she cummed all over his face and then he jumped up. Cleaning his face with the back of his hand.

"Where are you going?" She moaned out as he headed for the door.

"That's all I can give you. I don't want you to do anything you'll regret or even get in trouble for later." Before Kerry could reply, Derrick stormed out the door, closing it tight behind him.

"Damn!" Kerry murmured before turning over to sleep.

12

The delightful smell of bacon, butter biscuits and cheese grits creeped into Kerry's nostrils. Slowly, she rolled over to her side. The aching in her skull wouldn't allow her to move to quickly. "Awe," she moaned out in pain. Now she understood why they called it a hung over. She felt as if she was in a pool of pain. Slowly, she reached for her phone to check for miss calls. Bryan must be worried sick, she assumed. She looked at the phone and surprisingly there was no missed calls.

"This nigga must didn't go home his self." Kerry roared before throwing the phone back down onto the bed. As quickly as she could, she jumped up from the bed and fetched the bathroom. The hangover felt like a balloon under her cranium, slowly being inflated, pressure mounting. She splashed cold water onto her face just to feel something refreshing and instantly she wished she could wash her brain free of the toxins too. The mirror showed her eyes, no longer the glamour girl of last night, a mesh of glitter gold over the white. Once Kerry face was wiped clean of last night discretions she wobbled to the kitchen to fetch some of Alexus food. Only, Alexus didn't hear her coming. Frightened by Kerry's appearance, Alexus took in a sudden intake of breath and stumbled backwards, jamming her feet into the pantry door behind her.

"Awe!" she screamed as her shoulders shook in fear. It wasn't until she took another look at Kerry when she noticed it wasn't a stranger in her house.

"Where the hell you come from?" Alexus blurted out.

"From the back, I was in your guess room." Kerry's frighten expression matched Alexus. She knew Alexus was is the kitchen but when Alexus screamed, so did Kerry. Both their eyes were bulk wide as they pressed their hands against their chest while gasping for air.

"You been here the whole time?" Alexus asked before turning to flip the bacon in the skillet.

"Yes, you didn't know that?" Slowly, Kerry plopped down in the bar chair and rested her head on the granite island.

"No, girl. I had no idea. We must've both been fucked up. I thought your butt went home but then again I don't remember telling you bye, so, I should've known you were still here."

"I thought maybe buddy told you where I was." Kerry growled as she held her head tightly.

"Who is buddy, and why would he tell me?" Alexus asked.

"Johnathan friend, you know the one who helped me off the floor last night."

"Are you talking about Derrick?" Alexus snapped.

"Yeah, why you say it like that?" Slowly, Kerry lift her head from the island. The aching in her skull increased with her every move. She groaned like a baby bear.

"No reason."

"It didn't sound like no reason." Kerry replied.

"Anyway, after he helped me to the back he said he would let you know I was back there. So, I thought you knew I was here."

"Girl, no. I had no idea. That nigga didn't come tell me anything, but then again, he probably did, and I just don't remember. I was pretty fucked up."

"Well, why you don't look like it. You all put together and shit. Hair all fixed, clothes fitting, and I don't see not one sign of pain."

"That's because I'm not rookie. You knew to this shit, I'm true to this shit." Alexus joked.

"Well, I hope you cooked enough food because if not, I'm going have to eat yours." Kerry said.

"It's enough, but you're going to need to chug down a beer and an Aspin to get rid of that headache before you can even enjoy your food."

"Do you have some more beer?" Kerry asked while through her sew-in to reach her scalp for a good scratch.

"Nope, them motherfuckers drunk up everything girl."

"Shit!" Kerry mumbled. Just as she laid her head back flat on the island, there was a knock at the kitchen door. She and Alexus both turned their attention towards the glass double doors.

"What the hell is he doing here?" Alexus questioned as she hesitantly fetched the door.

"Shit, I don't know! Fuck I look a mess." Kerry whispered as she attempted to comb her wild hair down with her hands before Alexus opened the door.

"I'm sorry to intrude like this but I think it's been a miss up with our phones." Derrick stood nervously in the door waiting for Alexus to invite him in. For a long awkward minute, she just stared at him with a funny face.

"With who phone?" Alexus snapped with her nose tooted up.

"Oh, not your phone but me and Kerry's phone." Derrick stuttered.

"Oh ok, come in." Alexus said before stepping to the side clearing the door entrance.

"So, I got your phone?" Kerry asked.

"It appears that way. I woke up this morning trying to make a call and couldn't get in my phone. I then remembered I sat my phone down on the night stand before I laid you down." Kerry picked up the phone that she had been mistaking for hers and looked at the screensaver. Sure enough, it wasn't her phone. How could she not notice, she thought? The kids' picture had been her screensaver for months.

"Oh, you're right, this isn't my phone." Kerry said before passing Derrick his IPhone. Their phones were identical.

"I'm sorry, I hadn't noticed." Kerry said.

"Oh, it's cool." Derrick pocketed his phone and then pulled out a Corona beer and an Aspin from his opposite pocket.

"Here, I figured you would need this later." Kerry looked up to Derrick who towered over her, standing at Six-feet plus. He was beyond beautiful but in a manly sort of way, and he smelled heavenly.

"Well, aren't you convenient?" Alexus said as the two, Derrick and Kerry blushed, looking into each other's eyes. *Damn, he fineeee*, Kerry thought as her hormones secretly danced like a school girl. No one feature made Derrick so handsome, though his eyes came close. People often spoke of the color of eyes, as if that were of importance, yet his would be beautiful in any shade to Kerry. From them came an intensity, an honesty, a gentleness. Perhaps something she had once saw in Bryan eyes that she hadn't seen a minute. It was if Derrick great spirit and noble ways shined through his eyes.

Kerry could tell what his beautiful came from deep within; it made her crave his sloppy kiss. As he popped the Corona open with his strong hands, she fantasized about his hands following the curves of her body.

"Here, drink that and take that, and you should be good in a minute." He commanded.

"Okay, thanks."

"Oh, and I think you might want to check your phone. It's being ringing non-stop." Derrick said.

"It's probably her HUSBAND wondering where she is." Alexus sarcasm couldn't be blunter, but Derrick didn't pay her any mind. Instead, he did the one thing he knew would piss Alexus off even more than she appeared to already be.

"After you talk to your husband and clean yourself up, give me a call. We can go over them details about that job later." Kerry was completely lost for a minute. She'd never spoken to Derrick about a job, but she sure wished she had. She'd been feeling useless lately and a job opportunity didn't sound so bad. She looked into Derrick eyes, and before she could blow his cover, he gave her a sexy wink. *Ooooh, okay, he's lying... Duh, Kerry,* she thought before going along with the shenanigans.

"Oh, yeah, sure... I will. I'll do just that." With her lips tooted and her nose crinkled, Alexus side eyed the two and as soon as Derrick had disappeared out of sight, she blurted out, "You're playing with fire."

"What you mean?" Kerry asked with a dumbfounded look.

"Bitch don't play with me. You're everything but stupid. Bryan is going to kill your ass." Kerry rolled her eyes at Alexus and grabbed a script of bacon from the plate.

"Nobody is worrying about Bryan ass. Hell, he somewhere out there doing his own damn thing, not worrying about me." Kerry replied.

"Kerry Bryan loves you and you know that. I would give the world to have a man look at me the way he looks at you."

"Bryan has changed Alexus, I'm telling you. He's not the same man I married." Alexus slid the plate of food in front of Kerry and said, "You know what the problem is?"

"No, I don't. What's the problem Dr. Phil?" Kerry joked.

"You're chasing the twenty-Percent Bryan lacks but if you keep playing with fire, you're going to lose the eighty percent you already have and be stuck with that lousy twenty." Alexus made perfect sense, but Kerry couldn't let her know that, so she laughed the advice off and then jumped up from the island.

"Thanks, I'll keep that in mind Dr. Phil. Now, let me go call my eighty percent and tell him why I didn't make home last night." Kerry said on her way out the kitchen.

"Try not to lie too hard on me." Alexus voice carried out the kitchen and down the hall.

13

"Aunt where have you been? We've been worried sick about you. Why didn't you call or text us back? Was your phone dead or something?" Skylar rushed her aunt with questions as soon as she entered the house and spotted Kerry in the kitchen. Kerry wasn't surprised Skylar would be the first to drill her about her disappearance last night since most times she acted like she was the parent.

Nervously, Kerry unpacked meat from the freezer for dinner. "I'm fine, I stayed the night at Alexus. Dinner will be a little late tonight by the way. This meat has to unthaw."

"Oh, don't bother, uncle Bryan went out and bought us some Big Daddy." Just as Skylar spoke Bryan's name he entered the kitchen with dinner in his hand.

"You said she would be here when we got back." Skylar said to Bryan as she helped him unload the bags. Placing the plastic food trays full of soul food onto the table.

"We got you bake chicken, mac and greens." Skylar slid Kerry plate over to her and then pulled out her plate full of oxtails, cabbage and mac & cheese.

"How you get oxtails and I got bake chicken?" Kerry joked.

"Hey, that's what happens when you spend the night out." Skylar joked back. Everyone including Bryan's mother and the kids took their seat at the tables. A heavy silence settled over them, thicker than the uneasy tension in the atmosphere. Kerry unsettled eyes glanced unceremoniously around the kitchen as she tried to avoid eye contact with Bryan. His silence spoke volumes. He was clearly pissed and just waiting for the right time to explode.

Anytime he would look Kerry's way, she would Some shift uncomfortably in her seat. She grasped her sweaty, nervous hands under the tables, while tapping her feet on the hardwood floors.

"So, how was the party aunt?" Before Kerry could respond to Skylar she blurted, "Hold on, hold on… I got to take this." Quickly, Skylar grabbed her plate of food and her phone and zoomed out the kitchen. Donta call came at the worse time, Kerry thought as she was stuck in the kitchen with Claire and Bryan.

"You know it's time to get that girl some birth control." Claire said.

"She's not having sex, Skylar isn't like that." Kerry snapped.

"Would you know?" Kerry looked over at Bryan with a mug that could kill and said, "And what does that suppose to mean?"

"Exactly what it sounds like, would you know?" Bryan snapped back.

"Why wouldn't I know? I'm the first and only one who would know. So, don't try me Bryan. One night doesn't change a mother fucking thing.

"Okay, okay... You two." Claire chimed in and said.

"No, it's not okay. How dare he sit there and judge my parenting because I was out for one night. Hell, I need a break sometimes." Kerry increased tone irritated Bryan's soul and she took notice to his redden face. He was beyond pissed. When he turned at last to face Kerry there was no sight of a peace, not in his eyes or in track marks on his reddening face. His eyes were narrowed, rigid, cold, and hard.

In that moment Kerry knew they were far away from peace. She drew in a deep breath, preparing for the storm. His burning hard stare would last only as long as it took him to think of the most brutally cutting thing he could think of to win his compelling argument.

"A break and neglection is two different things. A parent needing a break is understandable but a parent disappearing in thin air without a call or text is a whole different ball game. I must've called you ten times. I didn't know what to think or do. I contemplated if I should call the police or not. Skylar was worried sick, and I even called Shaniya to see if she had talked to you and then she began to worry. Was it to hard to pick up the phone for five seconds?" Kerry chewed up her food as Bryan talked. She wasn't going to butt in because once she started, she planned to take victory.

"Damn, you need a break from your family that bad? What do you need a break from exactly? You don't work, so its not like..." Before Bryan dig his whole deeper, his mother chimed in and stopped him, "Let it go Bryan. Let it go, please." Claire said.

"Naw, let him talk Claire. Let him get it off his chest. I don't work, so its not like what, Bryan?" Kerry shouted.

"I'm just saying it was inconsiderate of you to not answer your phone or call. That's all I'm saying Kerry."

"Naw, you're definitely saying more Bryan." Bryan knew when Kerry slid her food away from her and stood up that things was about to escalate from bad to worse.

"I'll tell you what's inconsiderate, you promising me you're going somewhere and then canceling because you suddenly decided your ex-girlfriend needed you. You flaked on me for little miss thing and you have the nerve to call me inconsiderate. All you ever do these days is run out the house leaving me here with the kids and chores all day. Damn right I need a break! This was never my idea of a life, I gave it shot because you asked me to, or did you forget that?" Bryan knew he had crossed the lines and Kerry had very valid points. And just like that he was the villain and not the victim. *Damn*, he thought. "I set myself up for that," he mumbled as Kerry stormed out the kitchen.

14

Not long after Kerry got home from shopping and getting her hair done, Kerry is disturbed by the knocks on her room door. She doesn't rush to answer it. For starters, she knew it can only be Skylar or Bryan and she wasn't really speaking to either of them. Bryan was still in hot water about his choice of words, and he'd been sleeping on the sofa for a week now. Skylar had become super moody and boy crazy of the last couple of days and it was beginning to irritate Kerry's soul, so she wasn't really giving her attention either.

Her day had been filled with laughter and her mind was at ease. She didn't feel like ruining her good mood being bother with either of the two. The day with Alexus had been a nice one. Kerry wished she could've told Alexus why she was really getting dolled up instead of lying about a job interview in the a.m., but she knew Alexus would only judge her and try to talk her out of it. Alexus liked nothing about Kerry and Derrick talking and if she'd known that

Kerry was buying new clothes and getting her hair and makeup done for a date with Derrick, she would've probably done everything in her power to convince Kerry that she was making a huge mistake.

The person knocking at the room door began knocking harder, entirely too hard, while twisting on the door knob. Kerry instantly grew frustrated and snapped, "What? Damn, who knocking on my door like that?"

"It's me, I can't get in because the door is locked." Bryan yelled back.

"It's locked for a reason Bryan." Kerry mumbled while quickly hiding the shopping bags in the closet.

"Open this damn door girl!" As soon as the floor was clear of all Kerry's shopping bags, she calmly walked over to the door and opened it.

"I'm trying to get dressed." She said to Bryan as he pushed pass her and into the room.

"Why are you getting dressed? Where are you going on a weekday?" Bryan tossed the rented DVD's on the bed along with the pop corn and goobers.

"I'm to meet up with some peoples about this job offer." Kerry lied.

"Job offer?" Bryan questioned as he stared dumbfounded at Kerry while she continued to dress.

"Yes, job offer. You know, so I can get off my ass and do something around here." Irritable, Bryan shook his head and then plopped down onto the bed.

"Eww Bryan, get up! Why would you sit on the bed with your day clothes on?" Without a response, Bryan jumped up from the bed and then sat in the chair near the window.

"Are we still on this subject, Kerry?"

"No, we're not Bryan. I'm not talking about anymore and honestly, I'm not mad about it. I just wished you would've told me that's how you feel before getting mad with me."

"But I don't feel like that Kerry. I was only mad and trying to make you mad by saying anything. I love having you to come home to. I've never had a problem with taking care of my household. Never! It's not a burden." Kerry slid the black pencil skirt up over her curves, and then slid on a white sequin blouse, she couldn't believe it when she started to cry. She hadn't cried in front of Bryan in awhile and for the first time crying in front of him made her feel like a helpless girl.

"Why are you crying?" Bryan swiftly rushed to Kerry side to comfort her, but she quickly pushed him away. "I'm okay, you don't have to baby me. I'm fine, and I'm not mad you, I promise. I just need to get myself together." Kerry said before spraying three sprays of Bryans favorite perfume, *'Enjoy'* by Dior onto her neck and blouse.

"You're not okay Kerry, and or you wouldn't be crying. My words hurt you and I'm sorry. That' why I'm trying to make it up to you baby. I took days off this week, so I can spend time with you and the kids because I know I've been slacking off."

"I don't need your sympathy Bryan."

"You're my fucking wife, Kerry! What you mean, sympathy? I love you Kerry, don't be silly. If you want to work, I'll support you, but I want it to be because you want to work, not because you feel like you have to. Why didn't you tell me you were looking for work? I could help. What job are you going for?"

"I'll let you know if things go through. I don't want to speak about it too early." Kerry replied with a crack in her voice, between sniffles.

"Stay tonight and have movie night with us, the family and I will take off work and we can look for you work together." Bryan attempted to hug Kerry and again she bagged back.

"I have to do this on my own, Bryan. If you would've told me ahead of time maybe I would've tried to adjust my schedule to spend some time with you because Lord knows we haven't been on the same page lately, but I can't cancel, so I'll have to catch yaw later with the movie." Before Bryan could respond Kerry grabbed her purse and speedily strutted out the door. Bryan heart felt as if it was ripping in half. If this was what life was going to be like with Kerry working, he already didn't like it.

Kerry had been so undecided on if she should cancel the date or not that she was surprised to see how far she'd come. Already the cafe was in sight. There was nothing elaborate about it, no fancy fonts or white etching upon the glass. You could pick the whole thing up and send it back thirty years and it wouldn't look out of place. There weren't any tables with fancy umbrellas, just the uneven pavement baring the cracks of age.

Despite it being late in the afternoon, Kerry could still hear music from the inside, the kind of old R&B Bryan always played a little too loud for the neighbors liking. But Kerry plan wasn't to sit at the bar and chat with Derrick until the wee hours, she was going to have a drink and a bite to eat and leave. Derrick had already been in the cafe looking like he's been stood up, but he knew Kerry would be late, from the text she sent, and he replied, *he would wait proudly*. Suddenly, all her preparations for the night fled her mind like a scared child, her brain felt full of static like an old television set that's lost the signal. She stopped at the door. Part of her screamed to turn around, but the other half of her was curious to see what the night with Derrick would go like.

"Hey, are you waiting for someone?" Derrick slowly turned to face the familiar voice. Kerry looked stunning, even dressed as a good girl. None of her cleavage was out like the last time he saw her, and she barely showed any legs in the knee length pencil skirt but still she was flawless. And Derrick had vowed not to lose his cool like most of the men did in her presence at the party. She was that beautiful. But Derrick refused to be a lame for anybody, just because they look good. He looked at how rich her dark complexion was and tried to remind himself, *keep it together Derrick, she's just a girl*.

"Yeah, I been waiting on this shorty for a minute but I don't think she's coming so you can join me if you like." Derrick joked back before standing to hug Kerry. He could wrap his arms around Kerry's waist three times it was so tiny, which he loved most about her because she had told him over a long conversation that had over the phone that she was a new mother, and to him that meant she had good jeans. Her body had no problem bouncing back after birth.

"Really, so you're just going to invite another to your table that easily?" Kerry kidded, flashing her beautiful white smile.

"I mean, I was getting a little lonely sitting here." Derrick pulled out Kerry's chair for to sit and then he followed.

"Look at you, being a gentleman and everything."

"Oh, baby, I'm always a gentleman." He cockily replied before waving over the waiter.

"Well okay then. You're a different apple from the bunch."

"What you mean?" Derrick asked as Kerry chuckled at her own comment, gawking at the menu.

"Oh nothing, never mind me. I'm just talking, but you are different from Johnathan's usual crew. He crowds were usually rough around the edges. You know, bad boy types?"

"No, I don't know. Johnathan was an officer and as well as most of our friends."

"Yeah, being a police officer never stopped them from sinning and acting a fool. It just gave them a badge to hide behind." Kerry tone changed instantly, she was no longer giggling with her comment. She grew to love Johnathan eventually, but he wasn't always her favorite and she hated how him, and his home boys hid their wrong doing behind their badge, and then pretended to be stand up guys in public.

"True, you've told no lie there. But let's change the subject. I see you are not to kin to police. I'm scared to say another word your scowl is so intimidating." Kerry wrinkled her face with laughter once again. Derrick fake frighten face and extra dramatics tickled her. The fact that he was so manly and so strong but pretended to be intimidated by her tone, slightly turned Kerry on.

"Now, you be sure to get whatever you like. Don't worry about the price." Derrick joked again. There was hardly nothing on the menu over the price 20.00 and spending twenty was a big jump. You would have to order a meal, an entree, and an acholic beverage.

"Ooh, what a big spender you are?" Kerry joked back. Derrick flashed his sexy smile while dazing into Kerry's big beautiful oval brown eyes.

"Oh, look-a-there, you have a dimple." Kerry joked as she pinched Derrick face like she was his beloved grandma. And like a kid he continued to blush.

"It's cute on you."

"What's cute about it?" Derrick joked.

"Here you are this big manly guy with a sweet soft dimple. I think it's very attractive." Kerry explained.

"Well, who am I to argue with a compliment. Don't stop, keep them coming." Derrick jested. Kerry had no idea that Derrick was such a jokester, he had her laughing the entire night. For the first time in years, she felt alive and noticed. Which was strange because Bryan wasn't a bad husband and he'd always showered her with love but with so many traumatic events following their love, Kerry sometimes felt like his love was built on saving her. Maybe, Alexus was right, she assumed as she enjoyed her perfect night with Derrick.

Maybe, the twenty percent Derrick had to offer felt good to have because she had been missing out on it for so long. She wasn't sure, but she was hundred percent sure she wasn't going to do anything to jeopardize losing her marriage. The plan was to have a little fun, and then, get back to reality, back to her husband and kids. But as the saying goes, time flies when you're having fun.

Kerry had stayed out far pass the curfew she set for herself, and after so many drinks, it became harder for her to pull herself off Derrick. Had he not been a gentleman, Kerry's plan to keep things simple would've failed. In good spirit, Derrick discreetly followed Kerry to be sure she made it safe and then went on by his way.

If only things were that simple for Kerry. After convincing Bryan, she stayed out at a bar to have drinks afterward her meeting, to clear her mind, she then had to force herself to sleep. Trying her hardest to forget the good Derrick and his adoring charm.

15

"Skylar your word is---Bulimia..."

"Bulimia... B-U-L-I..." *Come on Skylar don't mess this up. Just finish the word.* Skylar thought as she fought for first place in the national spelling bee.

"Yes, we're waiting... Go ahead." Ms. Chancellor the second judge on the panel said but before Skylar could finish her word she rushed off the stage hurriedly covering her mouth with one hand and holding her stomach tightly with the other. Speedily, she ran to the girl restroom, locking herself in the stall. Her stomach contracted so violently that she had no time to reach the toilet bowl.

Chunks of food covered in the creamy chyme from her stomach were propelled into the air and splattered the tile and wall of the stall. She heaved again and once more the floor was sprayed. The vomit came up looking like clam chowder and smelling like acidic Cheetos. Now she could not move forward without stepping on her own puke and she was feeling even weaker than before. She sank to her knees and retched until only clear liquid was coming up.

Her throat felt sore from the stomach acid that was layering it and her mouth tasted of vomit. There was no-one to fetch her a glass of water or offer to clean up the mess. Though there were witnesses standing around judging her failure to cleanness.

"Goodness, you couldn't wait until you were over the toilet to spill out your dinner?" The captain of the Jaguars cheerleader team blurted.

"I hear when you can't hold your vomit and it uncontrollably spills out, you're pregnant." The Junior captain added before the team of girls burst into laughter.

"Wait, it can't be… You mean to tell me nerds get pregnant too. Oh my, and she's supposed to be the good girl." Another girl from the mean girl-click added.

"Well, you know what they about the good girls?"

"No, I don't what do they say Bridgette?"

"That they're usually badder than the bad girls." Again, the girls burst into laughter on Skylar's expense. She stayed tucked away into the stall listening quietly, patiently waiting for the girls to live before she existed. The stomach-acid stench of vomit filled her nostrils. She surveyed the mess with watery eyes and her stomach dry-heaved again.

Please Lord don't let me be pregnant, Skylar secretly prayed as she waited for the restroom to clear before she ran for cover.

Skylar: *Meet me at our spot... ASAP, its important.*

Donta: *Cool. Give me a minute. I got to come up with something to tell couch.*

For what seemed like the longest thirty minutes of her life, Skylar waited for Dontae on the abandon soccer field, near the woods. When he finally appeared, nothing she had practice saying could come up. She froze, and every time he asked her, "Man, what's wrong Skylar? You're scaring me." She just shook her head and said, "You promise you want be mad?"

"I can't promise you nothing until, I know what's going on Skylar." Dontae words weren't comforting enough, and Skylar could bring herself to say the two words that she believed would change the course of their relationship.

"Okay, I promise I want get mad." He finally said. "Now, what is it? If you don't tell me, I'm leaving."

"I'm pregnant," she blurted as she nervously tugged on her yellow Tommy Hilfiger t-shirt.

"How do you know? Did you take a test?" Dontae quickly replied before he began to pace back and forth.

"No, but I've been feeling very ill lately. I can't keep nothing down and my period is late."

"But, you haven't taken a test?" Dontae rushed back over to Skylar space to look her in her glistening eyes. He could tell she was scared out of her mind and so was he, but he knew he couldn't show her his fear, when she was terrified enough for the both of them.

"No, I haven't taken a test yet." Skylar finally murmured.

"Okay, let's not freak out about something we're not sure about."

"But, what if I am Dontae?" Aggressively, Skylar pulled back from Dontae grip.

"But, what if you're not?" he blurted back before chasing behind Skylar to grab her again.

"Listen, whatever the test says, I'm here. We'll figure shit out from there. But, we can't be stressing and shit. I hate stress. Let's just take this shit a step at a time." Tightly, Dontae held Skylar in his arms. The sweat and dirt from his practice uniform rubbed up against her clean attire as the two embraced each other closely.

"Okay, you're right. I'll take the test first, and then we'll go from there." Skylar said before turning Dontae loose.

"Okay, cool. Call me as soon as you know. I got to go because couch going to be looking for me soon, but we'll talk when I get home." Skylar nodded and then watched Dontae disappear across the field. She could barely wait to take the test, but at the same time she was afraid to take it.

Hands shaking like a branch on a tree, Skylar picked up the third pee-stick and like the other two, it read pregnant. She was indeed pregnant and in a whole lot of trouble. She could barely stomach the disgust Kerry was going to feel towards her when she found out. Kerry and the family had such high hopes for Skylar and she was aware that her being pregnant was going to change all of that. She picked up the phone to call Dontae and on the first ring he answered, "What did it say?" he instantly questioned.

"I'm pregnant Dontae." Skylar answered before bursting into crying.

"Quick crying, Skylar. Crying not going to change anything man, so you might as well stop all that. We going to be straight shawty. We going to be good. I got you, chill." As straight forward as Dontae words were, they were comforting to Skylar. Just to know he was on her side made all the difference in the world, and like he demanded she stop crying.

"We will talk though, just chill. We're going to be straight. Go lay down and get some rest."

"Okay, I'll talk to you tomorrow baby." Skylar hung up the phone feeling reassured that everything was going to be okay.

16

"4.5.6.7... Wait, Shaniya you are off count. Let's do over, back from the top!" Sierra whole attitude made no sense to anyone who didn't know her. At twenty-one she was psychologically still a child. The world revolved around her, she saw no points of view other than her own and was super intimidated by Shaniya because she was Brody's new girlfriend.

If anyone looked grumpy, she assumed they were mad with her, no other explanations occurred to her. Then she would become defensive and instantly take on bully activities. Shaniya knew just as well as the rest of the girls on the drill team that her 8-count was never off. In fact, she was one of the best dancers on the team if not the best one, but she didn't feel like indulging into heated debated with Sierra today. Sierra tantrums were legendary, the whole band could hear her when she was pissed and yelling about. But as long as no one was objecting her way she was like a well-mannered preschooler, eating cookies and playing on the computer.

"1.2.3.4.5... Shaniya, really?" Sierra snapped.

"I'm sorry, but I got to take this." Shaniya blurted out as she ran to the side to answer her phone.

"Hey aunt?" Shaniya answered.

"Hey Niya, what are you doing? Can you talk?" Kerry asked.

"I'm in practice but it's okay I can talk. Is everything okay. Where is Khloe?"

"Yes, everything is okay Shaniya, calm down. Why do you sound so paranoid? Is everything okay with you?" Shaniya suspiciously looked around to see who was watching her, and when she noticed no one was she quickly grabbed her bag and walked out of the gym.

"I think Wayne is out of jail aunt." Shaniya whispered into the phone.

"What?" Kerry heard Shaniya clearly, but she was confused on the sudden speculation.

"I think Wayne..."

"I heard what you said Shaniya but why do you think that?" Kerry asked.

"Everywhere I go, I feel like someone is following me. It's like they're torturing me or something. I don't, I can't explain it but it's like they want me to know that they are there." Shaniya continued to whisper because she couldn't be sure who was watching and listening to her.

"Why are you whispering? Where are you?" Kerry snapped.

"I'm leaving practice. I want to make it to my dorm before night fall because I can't see who's following me when it gets to dark."

"Shaniya, it's already dark."

"I know, I didn't realize it got so late. My captain is in bitch mode and she's been working us to death."

"Shaniya, I want you to talk to somebody baby. You've been through a great amount of pain and I think is time you talked someone about it."

"Aunt, there is nothing wrong with me. I'm losing my mind or making this up!"

"I didn't say you were Shaniya, but you still need to talk to someone about everything you've been through. Including losing your mother. Both you and Skylar actually."

"Oh, my goodness, I should've never brought it up to you." Instantly, Shaniya eyes began to water. She badly wanted to cry but she didn't, she just listened to Kerry preach about her warfare.

"I'm glad you are telling me how you feel. Don't ever not tell me, especially with you so far away from me. I was going to suggest you see a therapist far before you mentioned someone following you. And I'm not saying that I don't believe you. Someone might be following you.

What's the chances of it being Wayne... I don't know but until we figure out who, I'm going to need you to not walk home by yourself anymore. Where is Brody?" Kerry roared.

"He got practice to, but anyway, I'll be fine. What was it you were calling about?"

"Don't dismiss me, Shaniya. I will hurt your feelings little girl." Kerry snapped, and she would probably say more if she could see the irritable faces Shaniya was making while she spoke.

"Anyway, you need to figure out what you're going to do for Khloe's birthday and let me know because I don't want to do no last-minute stuff."

"Okay, I'll let you know. I haven't figured it out yet, but I'll let you know soon." Shaniya fixed the irritation in her voice. The thought of celebrating Khloe's birthday changed her entire mood.

"Well call me when you figure it out. Do I need to stay on the phone with you until you make it to your dorm?"

"No, I see a couple of my friends. I'm just going to catch up with them really quick." Shaniya lied. She decided worrying Kerry about her safety would only make things worse. She would just have to deal with whoever was tormenting to her on her own. Quickly, she pulled her pair of grey swear pants out the bag and her grey hoodie. Walking home in her practice leotard wasn't such a good idea. She assumed whoever was watching her was most likely a man and her showing skin would probably only make things worse. Swiftly, Shaniya began to walk to her dorm and for a minute she believed everything was fine. She hadn't seen or heard anyone, that's until she was alone in the alley that led to the back of the dorm.

She turned to face the creepy sound of footsteps and her heart sank right through her skin onto the concrete ground she walked on. Yet, again, she saw no one, but she heard their steps growing closer and closer. In seconds she ran to the dorm door and started pulling on it. The stranger was now whispering her name, "Shaniya…" She didn't bother turning around because she knew she wouldn't see him. Instead she nervously rambled through her purse for her keys to the dorm. Shaniya had assumed coming to the back door would be best since it was hardly ever locked, but sure enough her luck was bad, and the door was indeed locked for the first time in months.

Suddenly, Shaniya couldn't breathe, it felt as if someone was choking her. Her heart was racing and all she wanted to do was curl up into a ball and wait for someone to save her. But no one would, no one was there. A choked cry for help forced itself up her throat, "Help me, somebody please!" As she cried out for help she felt a tear drop run down her cheek. His whispers grew closer and louder, "Shaniya… Shaniya… It's just me and you. No one can help you." The stranger response to Shaniya cry for help assured her this was real, she was being purposely chased and she wasn't tripping like Kerry had suggested. Someone was after her. It seemed as if this was the end of the road for her. When Shaniya couldn't find her key, she turned around to face the man who in the darkness, "Fuck you! You don't scare me." She cried out with tears dripping down her cheeks. Her voice echoed through the alley, scaring the birds from the trees.

"I'm not running anymore. Come on, come and get me!" Suddenly, Shaniya heard no one. The whispers were gone. She turned to bang on the door again, hoping someone would come open the door but no one came, and just as she turned to walk away her frenemy Kayla startled her with her presence. It was as if she appeared from thin air. Shaniya heartbeats pound like thunder ripping from her chest.

"Who were you talking to Shaniya?" Kayla asked as she watched tears storm from Shaniya glistening eyes.

"Nobody don't worry about it." Shaniya snapped before walking away.

"If you needed to get in, come on. I got my key." Kayla yelled out before Shaniya could disappear down the alley. Shaniya hesitantly thanked Kayla before speedily strutting through the dorm.

"No need you're good." Kayla replied before stopping Shaniya in her tracks with one tap on the shoulders, "Listen I know we not the best of friends, but I also know you've been through some things Shaniya. Some horrific things that no one should have to go through. Maybe, you should talk to someone, and I say this with love, not to be funny or anything. I mean it's nothing to be ashamed of. The only thing that wouldn't be normal is you not talking to someone." Shaniya could feel Kayla sincerely concerned for her and maybe she was genuine with her advice, but Shaniya couldn't that chance trusting her again. After Kayla had betrayed her trust, telling all their friends about her dealings with an older man, Wayne. Shaniya had confided in Kayla one night about Wayne. She was a freshman and she was very lonely. She'd squared Kayla to secrecy but that didn't mean anything to Kayla when she needed to get in good with the in-crowd.

Shaniya had thanked God she didn't Kayla everything about Wayne. She had left the juiciest parts out, telling only what she felt would make her popular; Living her best life in Miami as a teen. She bragged about the riches and money, but she never told Kayla about the deceit and murders.

"Thanks. I'll take that in consideration." Shaniya lied before walking off. She knew she was tripping and talking to someone would only suggest otherwise.

"Well, it was good seeing you." Kayla blurted out to Shaniya as she walked away. Shaniya didn't bother to respond. She just through up her hand and kept it moving.

17

For the first time since starting college, Shaniya found herself alone. Cast off in the back of the library with her head buried into the books like a natural nerd. she sat alone and completely alert of her surroundings. Since the melt down she had neglected her social life a bit. She wanted to be alone so that she could think and piece together the strange events that had been happening in her life. She'd missed Brody, but she didn't feel like explaining to him her fears, knowing he would just think she was losing her mind like Kerry and Kayla assumed.

It was moments like these that Shaniya missed her mother the most. Khloe was the best supporter and comforter. Shaniya knew if her mother was alive she would never be alone to face such horror by herself. For weeks, Shaniya lived in her own little world. Neglecting all her social activities; drill team, beta club, and Brody. She'd adopted a daily routine that didn't include interacting with people. She only dealt with people the four days she worked the diner waitressing. She would bring home food from the diner, then retire in her dorm to study and off to sleep. This was her daily regimen until the weekend, and then she would slide in some time at the library to get fresh air and a different scenery to study.

As she flipped through the pages of her economics book, she felt the heat of someone eyes piercing through her skin. She slowly looked up, hoping to be discreet and bumped eyes with Brody. His eyes seemed to have passion burning inside of them. She sat there shy and embarrassed at a table across the room from where he was standing at a book-case flipping through some pages, and she could feel her panties becoming damp from the growing desire to feel him inside her. Shaniya hadn't realized how much she'd missed Brody until she saw him.

He'd begged her to open up to him about whatever she was going through but she didn't. Shaniya bluntly told Brody that she was going to need space until she could figure out some things, and although Shaniya assured Brody it wasn't him or nothing he'd done, he still couldn't help believe he'd failed her somehow. He called she didn't answer, if he entered a room she was present in, she'd would leave, and the behavior continued to Shaniya felt Brody got the picture; she wanted to be alone.

She crossed her legs and moved them back and forth, creating alight friction against her vagina and making her desire even more intense. She didn't realize that she was sucking on the eraser of her pencil and staring at him until she felt him staring back. Shaniya moved her eyes up from where they had locked on the bulge of Brody penis to his face, and for what seemed like an endless moment, their eyes met. Brody broke the stare and frowned at her. It was then remembered how his arrogance turned her on. She yearned to draw his bottom lip into her mouth, but she knew from his mug it wasn't possible. Clearly, he'd finally grown impatient, waiting on her to let him back into her life.

She looked back down at the economics book she was studying for a brief moment, contemplating if she should go over and make conversation with Brody, maybe even apologize for cutting him off so cold. When Shaniya looked up, he was gone. Her heart dropped to her stomach, *he doesn't love me anymore*, she thought before a single tear dropped from her gleaming eyes.

She scanned the library quickly, and then she noticed him leaving the out the side door. She felt as if shew as a second away from breaking down and crying in a public library wasn't an option, so Shaniya quickly jumped up from the table, snatching up her books, denim jacket, and purse and then ran out the same side door. Before she could inhale the fresh air, she was snatched up. Tightly, a hand covered her mouth. Shaniya scream told a story of pain within, and confusion.

"Let me go," she mumbled. His rough hands scrapping her lips as she wiggled restless to free herself of his grip. He inhaled her lovely scent as he tussled to stiff her body from behind. Tightly, he hugged her body closely to his chest, wrapping his arms around her waist, lifting her body with one hand. As soon as Shaniya feet left the ground, she instantly felt helpless and begin to cry.

"Stop crying, I'm not going to hurt you." Gently, he tossed her in the unfamiliar Ram truck and buckled her into the seat belt.

"Brody!" Shaniya screamed. Finally, she could see his face.

"You scared me, I thought someone was trying to kidnap me. Don't fucking do that! You don't know what I'm going through already." Brody listened to Shaniya nag as he walked around the truck. As soon as he jumped in the driver seat, he snapped, "I would know if you told me, and I'm sorry if I scared you. I just knew if I ask you to get in, you would've come up with some excuse not to." Shaniya head jerked, almost smashing into the dash board, Brody took off so fast.

"Brody, slow down!" She blurted as she held onto the door for stability.

"I really don't have time for this. Stop the car so I can get out, please."

"No, I'm stopping until we talk." Brody replied as he slowly approached the red light. Quickly, Shaniya tried to snatch open the door, but it wouldn't open. She then smashed on the unlock button, but it wouldn't click.

"It's on child safety, Shaniya." Brody said. The calm in his voice irritated Shaniya but she knew there was only way to get rid of Brody. She had to give him what he wanted; a conversation, an explanation, and even a little attention. He was too popular to be dumped the way

Shaniya had dumped him, so he needed closure or something to make him feel like he was in control of the break-up.

"I'm sorry for the way I broke things off, Brody. I really meant what I said when I said it wasn't you but me. I got some things going on in my life that I can't really speak about or explain, and I just didn't want to burden you with my problems." Brody listened while Shaniya spoke. He didn't murmur a word, he just listened and drove.

"I miss you just as much as you miss me, but I got to do what's best for me right now. I got a daughter depending on me and if I'm not good, she's not good."

"I hear you Shaniya and I understand but it's not your call to make decisions for me. I never said you were a burden. All I've been trying to do is to get you to open up to me so that I could help you through everything you've been going through."

"But I don't want your help, Brody!" Shaniya snapped as she instantly grew frustrated.

"Okay, cool. I'll leave you to your business, but can we just please get away for a weekend. Me and you, leaving all problems behind until we return and if you still want to go your own way from there, I won't stop you." Shaniya looked over at Brody with the evil eye. He just wouldn't give up and his persistent irritated Shaniya's soul.

"Roll your eyes if you want but I already had this trip planned and its paid for and I don't won't to not go because you mad about nothing."

"Okay Brody, shit. I'll go! Wait, where are we?" Shaniya looked around the neglected the park. It was secluded on a dead-end road.

"I want some." Brody replied arrogantly.

"What? You done lost your mind." Shaniya blurted before bursting into laughter.

"I'm not about to fuck you in no park, Brody. Take me back to the school." Brody ignored Shaniya request. Instead he unbuckled his belt, then reached over and began kissing Shaniya like she was his last super. She wanted to stop him, but she couldn't. She didn't have the will-power. Once he started massaging her breast it was over, there was no turning back. She had been stressed for past few weeks and her body were very tense. Brody touches was very much needed.

In no time Brody had Shaniya distressed denim jeans and white t-shirt on the floor. All was left was her bra and panties and he moved the panties to the side and pulled up the bra for visual on her breast. The two fucked like two hot rabbits, rocking the truck. One time wasn't enough, so they went three rounds before returning to the dorms.

18

The first time Derrick laid eyes on Kerry he knew he wanted her. He wanted to feel her insides, to caress her body and her fill her up with his seeds. The first time they kissed he thought he would lose control of his hormones, but he didn't. Two months and several dates later, he stilled possessed control. They had yet to make love. Partly because he had much respect for Kerry to wait and partly because the thought her wiping him off just to go lay with her husband angered him.

Derrick didn't know how long he was going to be able to see Kerry without invading her vagina walls, but he knew anytime she was in his presence, he felt alive and when she wasn't in his presence, he thought about her. She invaded his every thought. He dreamed of her doing freaky things to him all the time, whether he was stuck in rush-hour traffic or working out in the gym. The mere thought of her made him arouse.

Every time Derrick saw Kerry he tried to make it special. He wanted to her think about him when he wasn't around the way he thought about her.

Ducked off in a suit deep into the woods away from the city, the two enjoyed each other's company. The hotel was comfy with an old school feel to it. Which made the night more romantic in Kerry eyes? Slow music played from Derrick's playlist onto the portable speakers. His style of music was old skool; everything from R-Kelly to Aretha Franklin. If it was a hit back in the day, he had it on his play list. The sipped wine around the vanilla scented candles. They talked about everything from goals, sports, and fantasies.

"So, you mean to tell me you don't have a fantasy?" Kerry teased Derrick.

"No, I don't believe in all that junk." Derrick lied.

"Is it one girl you would like to have in your bed, famous or regular, doing whatever you like most in the heat of the moment?" The first name popped up in Derrick's mind was Kerry, but he lied and said, "Nope, I'm telling you. I'm not into all that overrated erotica mess."

"Well if you were mine, and I wasn't happily married, we would lie in my bed butt-naked, slow music on, much like right now but instead we would be caressing each other's bodies. Then I would prop myself up on a pillow and dip my nipple into a glass of wine and hold my breast, letting you suckle the wine off it. I would do the same with my other nipples and feed it to you." As Kerry recited her fantasy to Derrick her vocals changed. She from silly goofy Kerry to sexy seductive Kerry and Derrick could barely take it. He tried his best to act hard but when Kerry started rubbing on her long shiny legs he started to lose control, and without knowledge he was slightly drooling from the corner of his mouth.

"If I was aloud to have my way, I would rub up and down the shaft of your dick until he stretched out in the palm of my hand. I would choke it repeatedly until your precum dripped lightly from the hole. I would rub my fingers across the tip and then suck your juices off my fingers." Softly, Kerry massaged her vagina under the pink maxie dress. Derrick couldn't take it anymore, and just as Kerry assumed he would, Derrick crawled over to the sofa on his knees to kiss Kerry awaiting pussy. Slowly, and gently he kissed her vagina through her panties in circular motion. He kissed her lips as if they were the lips on her face, very passionate and when he couldn't take it no more he slid her panties to the side for a real taste.

Just as Kerry felt his tongue flicker inside her pussy walls she said, "Stop." And pulled him away. "That was just my fantasy. It's nothing I can make real." Kerry jumped from the sofa, pulled down her dress and grabbed her purse.

"I'll see you later, Derrick." Like a fool caught red handed with his hand in the cookie jar, Derrick sat on the floor with looking dumbfounded with his dick standing at attention.

"Where you going, Kerry? You don't have to go." He said before she unlatched the door.

"But I do, I have to get home to my kids and husband. You understand, don't you?" Derrick wanted to be a gentleman and understand but his hormones didn't. He wanted to rip Kerry to shreds and fuck her like a mad dog.

"I mean, I guess understand." He stuttered.

"I know you do." Kerry replied before slamming the door behind her. During the entire ride home, she thought about Derrick and how he probably would've been the best fuck of her life. She badly wanted to try him out, but Alexa's Tyler Perry borrowed advice was stuck in her head, *don't lose your eighty percent chasing after the twenty percent you don't have.*

Kerry vagina tickled for affection and she couldn't wait to get home to take her sexual frustration out on Bryan. Five to six songs later, she arrived home. Before pulling into the driveway she turned the headlights off, to avoid waking up the house. It was late, and she just wanted to slip in and head straight to the shower and she did. Bryan was fast asleep, at least that's what Kerry assumed. Since he seemed passed out when she passed him in the bed.

Quietly, he stood in the door watching Kerry shower. Apart of him wanted to scream where the hell you been all night? But the larger part of him just wanted to jump in the shower with her. He gawked at her sexy silhouette through the frosted glass as he contemplated on his next move; should he join her or return to bed. Before he could decide, Kerry sexily mumbled, "Come on, get in. Don't just watch." Bryan was shocked to know Kerry knew of his presence. Slowly, he stripped from his Ralph Lauren pajamas. As soon as he entered the shower, he lifted her up against the wall and she straddled her legs around his waist as he buried his tongue into her mouth.

As they devoured each other Kerry thought about Derrick and the way his lips felt against hers. The more she thought about Derrick the hotter she got for Bryan. Water cascaded down both of their bodies, Kerry could feel the head of Bryans dick rubbing up against her fine hairs. His hard body felt so good up against her petite frame. He was no Derrick, but he was just as strong as a man Derrick size.

"Fuck me, Bryan." Kerry demanded before pulling Bryan in closer to her body. She could feel the head of his dick invade her pussy walls, and then his entire dick was inside her. She wanted it so bad, Kerry almost nutted instantly. She started kissing him deeply and palming the back of his head.

"Fuck me baby, this is your pussy." She moaned. Bryan had been pleading for Kerry to take charge and talk dirty to her in the beginning of their marriage, but she assured him, that wasn't her thing. She thought it was lame and a big turn off but tonight, it was everything she wanted. She shouted out all the nasty things she wanted to tell Derrick and Bryan loved every bit of it.

"Fuck this pussy right or you want get another chance." Deeper and deeper, Bryan shoved his dick into his wife, trying his best to keep up with her needs. They two fucked for a good half hour in the shower and then he finally came. Kerry could feel his hot cum shoot up inside her. They got out the shower and Bryan thought they would dress and cuddle, but Kerry was still hot and horny. She rode Bryan dick all night like she was practicing for a marathon.

19

Every year on Khloe's birthday Shaniya felt like she died a little more. Every year it was a reminder of her that her mother was missing some of the most precious times in her kids and grandchild life. Shaniya gawked at her happy daughter with her sparkly eyes as Khloe about with her friends. She looked just like her grandmother but with her father's complexion. Shaniya could feel her heart sank in as she imagined her mother and her daughter celebrating their birthday's together. Their special days was only five days apart. The thought that Khloe would never know her grandmother crushed Shaniya's soul, but she had to shake the sadness for her baby's sake.

Khloe and Bryan Jr. and their friends ran around like wild animals in the zoo. It was safe to say the circus themed party was a success. The kids interacted with the animals good and no one, not one child feared the clown. Maybe because he was too skinny. He looked more goofy than scary, which was a plus. He wore a striped shirt like he'd just broken out of some cartoon jail and his arms were like flexible toothpicks. The only thing right about him was his abnormally large hands and feet - great for catching baseballs if he'd got the co-ordination. He walked like his legs object to the weight of his feet, like one of his parents was a penguin. Khloe started to snicker and point and as usual that started a contagion in the gang - everyone began to laugh with her. In the end Khloe was glad she hired him, he was just naturally funny.

"Why are you sitting over here in the corner all ducked off?" Shaniya walked over to the food table where Skylar was stationed.

"I'm just trying to keep these kids from knocking over this table. One little boy already tried to pick the cake up."

"And where was he going to take it?" Shaniya asked with a huge grin on her face.

"Girl, I have no idea, your guess is better than mine."

"Are you okay? You look like you're going to fall out." Shaniya asked Skylar as she struggled a little with her balance. The music was so loud that it made her skin tingle. It felt as if a loud band lived in her head. The bass thumped in time with her heart beat as though they were one, filling her from head to toe with music. She'd liked the song playing; *Uptown funk* by Bruno Mars but she couldn't take the loud noise and nausea feeling at the same time. Over the roar of music, a distant, loud chant could be heard. Kerry, Alexus and their friends were cheering for Skylar to come show the kids some dance moves. Skylar couldn't utter one any words, or else she would vomit all over the place. She tried her best to keep still hoping the bile would go down instead of up and out but after few seconds, she noticed the feeling was getting better. She would vomit rather she wanted to or not. Quickly, she ran into the house, up the stairs and into her bathroom.

"Khloe scared aunt Skylar up with them dance moves. She didn't even want to battle you baby." Shaniya joked trying to defer the attention from Skylar dramatic exit. Laughter rang in her ears and it wouldn't seem to stop. Khloe demanded more and more of her mother's attention and the song that they danced to seemed to go on for eternity. Shaniya intention was to go check on Skylar, but the music got louder, and the songs got better one pick after another and Khloe wouldn't let go of her mother. She pulled Shaniya into the center the yard and wouldn't let go. Shaniya had no choice but to join the crowd of hyper kids, jumping in a huddled group like Tic-Tacs being shaken in a box.

Khloe twirled around in her beautiful colorful tutu like she was the star ballerina of the night. At four years old, she knew what it meant to be stylish, Kerry and Shaniya made sure of that. Her hair bows never not matched her outfit and she was always dressed in the cutest girl's fashion. For her birthday she was sporting a handmade purple and green tutu and custom shirt that read; It's a princess birthday. Her hair ribbon and bows coordinated with her outfit and so did her cute little airmax and lace socks. Kerry might've moved up in the world, but she still had some hood in her and it showed in the way she dressed both Khloe and baby Bryan.

"Shaniya, where did Skylar go?" Kerry yelled across the yard.

"I don't know, that's a good question." Shaniya replied as she looked around to see if Skylar had return. Easily she had forgotten that Skylar was gone. With so much going on with the party her attention was everywhere.

"Well go see if you can find her so we can sing *happy birthday* to Khloe." Kerry yelled back.

"Okay aunt... Khloe, let me go find aunt. I'll be back okay?" Shaniya kneeled her to kiss her daughter before disappearing from the party. When she found her little sister, she was stretched out across her bed looking like a sick puppy.

"Oh lord..." Shaniya said as soon as she entered the room. "I know that look." She added before plopping down next to Skylar on the bed.

"Oh lord, what?" Skylar snapped.

"You're pregnant, aren't you?" Shaniya rolled Skylar over to her back so that she could see her stomach.

"Why you say that? No, I'm not pregnant!" Quickly, Skylar rolled back over to hide her still tiny frame.

"Girl, yes you are. You've never been a good liar and right now, you're lying. I'm not no damn dummy, I've been there done that, remember?" Shaniya snapped back.

"Do aunt know about this?"

"No, and I'll like to keep it that way." Skylar shouted.

"And for how long do you think that's going to last, Skylar?"

"For as long as you keep your mouth shut."

"I'm not going to lie to you, and I'm going to tell but I will give you a chance to do it first." Shaniya said.

"Some sister you are." Skylar sat up on the bed and tears began to drop from her eyes.

"I know I might seem cruel to you right now, but I promise you, I'm only thinking about you. This is not something you want to go through alone, Skylar. I promise you it's not." Like a baby, Skylar broke down into full sobbing. She tucked her head into the pillow in front of her so that her crying wouldn't be heard.

"I know you're scared, and yes aunt is going to be pissed as she has every right to. You know you were supposed to be careful. Shit, I didn't even know you were fucking. Why wouldn't you tell me that Skylar?" Skylar beautiful healthy hair swung freely as she shook her head, "I don't know. I guess I was to ashamed to talk about the decision with anyone."

"I'm your sister girl. These are the things we suppose to talk about together. I would told you how to avoid this situation. Who's better to tell you than me." Skylar tears increased. She was beyond embarrassed of her situation, even talking to her sister about it felt odd. Shaniya had always been the experienced one, the more mature one of the two. Close family and friends had always expected Shaniya to do the most frowned upon things but not Skylar. She was the scholar, the good kid who always seek peace, the kid who everyone had high hopes for and now she was a teen pregnant with another teens baby.

"You got to tell aunt."

"You said that already, Shaniya." Skylar replied between her muffles. "She's going to kill me, man. Can't we just wait awhile?"

"Of course, she's going to be super mad at first, but she'll get over it and when she does, she'll be your biggest supporter. The shoulder you're going to need to lean on throughout this whole ordeal. Plus, what's waiting going to do, besides prolong the consequences. The anticipation alone would run you crazy. You should want to get it over with. Are you listening to me?" Shaniya shouted as she lifted Skylar head from the pillow to look into her sorrowful eyes.

"Yes, I hear you. Lets just get this over with. I rather do it while you're here." Skylar jumped up from the bed and slid back on her airmax Nike shoes that was the same color and style as Khloe's. All the girls, Khloe, Kerry,

Shaniya and Skylar dressed alike for the big day. Instead of the girls wearing tutu's like Khloe, they wore dark blue denim jeans and their shirts were all customized to cater to Khloe. Kerry and Skylar shirt read; I'm the birthday girl's aunt. Shaniya shirt read; it's my little princess birthday today.

"Okay, well maybe we'll tell her after the party. Right now, they're about to sing *happy birthday* to Khloe." Shaniya said as she followed Skylar down the stairs.

"Where yaw going?" Kerry yelled from the kitchen as she watched both Shaniya and Skylar trail to the back yard.

"Oh, we thought you were outside. We were about to meet you, so we could sing *happy birthday* to Khloe." The girls doubled around to the kitchen.

"I been looking for yaw for the last thirty-minutes. We already done sang to Khloe and fed the kids cake. You know it's getting late and people got to get their kids home." It was clear Skylar that Kerry had grown irritable with her and Shaniya. Skylar knew her aunt like she knew her favorite book and she knew Kerry had an attitude because she felt it was irresponsible for them to disappear from the party. If that made her frustrated Skylar could only imagine what her news was going to do to her aunt mood.

"Well, we had a little situation. I'm sorry we didn't hear you calling us."

"What kind of situation?" Claire asked as she help Kerry put away things from the party.

"Aunt, I'm going to tell you something, but can you promise to keep your cool and talk things out?" Kerry paused for a few seconds and gently sat the dish she was drying down onto the table.

"What have you done now, Shaniya?" Kerry asked suspiciously. Shaniya had grasped both Claire and Kerry's attention and neither of them was cleaning anymore. Their eyes fixated on Shaniya as they waited for to spill the tea.

"I said promise you will keep your cool?" Shaniya said.

"So, basically, you want me to lie to you, because I can't promise something like that if I don't know what's going on."

"She promises, she will keep her cool. I'll make sure of it." Claire added. The suspense was killing her. Since Kerry and Bryan's marriage, she'd grown fun of the idea of having grandkids and she badly wanted the girls to acknowledge her as their grandmother. Which was very difficult for them to do since she wasn't all that fun of Bryan taking in so much responsibilities in the beginning of he and Kerry's relationship. Claire initially felt Bryan deserved a girl with less baggage.

"Okay... Here is it is..." Shaniya said, but before she could finish her sentence, Skylar spilled her own beans, "I'm pregnant aunt Kerry." Shocked, Kerry immediately plopped down into a chair. She looked as if she could barely breathe.

"Aunt are you okay?" Skylar asked as she walked closer to Kerry to check on her health.

"Kerry pressed her hand to her chest. It was if she was having a heart attack.

"Aunt... Say something?" Shaniya nagged as she sat down beside her Kerry. For a few seconds everyone was quiet, except the kids laughing and playing about in the living room.

"How could you be so careless, Skylar how?" Skylar stood still with tears dripping from her distressed eyes. She was speechless. There was nothing she could say to rectify her choices. She knew better and that was facts. There was no way around it. Kerry stared at Skylar for as long as she could waiting for an answer, but Skylar never murmured a word.

"I guess you were right. She is having sex." Kerry stood up and said to Claire.

"Oh... I don't want to be right about such things Kerry. Honestly, it doesn't even matter who's right or wrong now. We just must pull together and make best of things. Support at times like this is a must." Skylar wasn't sure how Claire knew about her having sex, but she was thankful that she was there to keep Kerry calm.

"I can't deal with this right now." It was clear Kerry was a blink away from crying.

"I wanted your mother to be proud of how I raised her kids and now I don't know what she must think of me. I pray I haven't disappointed her on her birthday." Kerry managed to say through her burning throat.

"Aunt is not your fault. You've done great with us." Skylar cried out to Kerry as she walked away.

"You broke my heart Skylar, you broke my heart." Kerry murmured back as she disappeared down the hall.

20

The night rolled over bringing a threat of a storm. Light was covered by the rapidly falling night. The bright blue sky transformed into an ocean of blackness. Shimmering stars illuminated the moonless, jet black sky, as if to remind Skylar that even in darkness there is still light. The air was still, and heavy, thick clouds covered half the sky. A cool breeze swept the alienated street. Owls swept silently overhead. Even shadows were swallowed by the encroaching darkness.

Furious, Skylar rocked back and forth in the rocking chair. For hours, she'd been on the porch waiting for Dontae to return her call. He'd promised to call her back once he was home from practice, but he hadn't. Skylar had blown his phone up, calling repeatedly until he finally turned his cell phone off, and when she called his house phone he hung up quickly pretending he was attending to some important business that he couldn't discuss at the moment.

Dontae words, "I got you," repeated in Skylar's head as she thought about his actions. Nowhere did his actions bag up his words. He didn't have Skylar, instead he'd been dodging the conversation about the baby and her since she gave him the news.

"Lying cowardly bastard." Skylar murmured before she jumped up from the rocking chair. Speedily, she walked to Kerry old Nissan Murano. She'd snuck the keys while Kerry was sleeping. She figured Kerry wouldn't miss the car since she was had her new shiny BMW. Quickly, Skylar jumped in the car and sped out the parking lot before anyone could notice. She'd only drove a couple of times and that was with Kerry supervision, but that didn't stop her. She had to see Dontae. She needed to look him the eyes to get the answers she needed. Even if that meant pissing Kerry off, having a wreck or being pulled over by police.

Skylar drove like she was a mad woman, Vin Diesel skills had nothing on her. Within 15-minutes she had arrived at Dontae's house. Hurriedly, she sped into the nice brick driveway. She didn't care about the scene she was causing either. The way she figured if his mother was home, it was a good time to fill her in on her son's good news and if she wasn't home, she would hear about the disturbance from her nosey ass neighbors. Either way, Skylar was determined to make Dontae face the music one way or the other.

Aggressively, she banged on the door, covering the peek hole with one hand. It took what seemed like forever for Dontae to come to the door, and when he did he was shocked to see that it was Skylar who'd been beating on the door.

"Skylar?" He said.

"What's the matter baby, you don't look to happy to see me." Skylar said before pushing pass Dontae, barging into the house.

"Naw, I wasn't expecting you. How did you get here, Skylar?" Skylar didn't bother answer any of Dontae answers, instead walked around the house like a detective looking for a murder weapon.

"Why haven't you been answering my phone calls Dontae?" Skylar asked as she checked the coat closet for hidden guest.

"I told you I been busy, and what the hell is you looking for?" Dontae shouted. "There is no one here," just as Dontae lied, Chantel the co-captain of Douglas high school cheerleader team appeared at the top of the circular stair case.

"Really, Dontae? Really?" Skylar shouted. Dontae could shit bricks. He'd been firm with Chantel when he told her not come out the room, as he thought his mother had lost her and returned home.

"Yeah, really Dontae?" Chantel said. "Is this why you asked me to stay in the room, so you can talk to this bitch?" Chantel pointed her finger and tooted her nose up at Skylar as if she was nothing.

"Oh, I'm not going to be disrespected by your whores, that's what's not going to happen!" Quickly, Skylar ran up the stairs after Dontae's side piece and before he could catch up with her, Skylar she had already attacked Chantel. The two girls grunted as they took handfuls of each other's clothing and hair and attempted to wrestle the other to the ground. Then the Skylar released Chantel's shirt and used that hand to start upper-cutting Chantel in the face. Skylar then brought Chantel face down her hair so that she could knee her in the face. Blood flowed from Chantel's broken nose and she staggered backwards as Dontae pulled them apart.

"Skylar stop girl! You are tripping." Dontae shouted before Skylar struck him.

"I'm tripping? But you the one here with a bitch, ignoring my calls and shit, but I'm tripping!" Forcefully, Skylar charged Dontae. She pounded on him like he was her property, hitting him everywhere his hand couldn't cover.

"Stop girl, you pregnant. Chill out, Skylar!" Dontae yelled as he attempted to run from Skylar's reign.

"You mean to tell me you got a fucking a baby mama and shit and you got me all up in your bed?" Chantel screamed out as she pinched her nose to stop the dripping blood.

"I'm not just his fucking baby momma, I'm his fucking girl!" Skylar yelled back as she continued to strike Dontae.

"You know what, I don't have time for this shit. I'm gone. If I were you I would be doing the same thing girl, but I didn't know he had a girl. He told me, he was single." Skylar stop a few seconds to turn and face Chantel, "I believe you, how would you know when he around here acting like he single and shit."

"Man, she is lying. She knew damn well I told her I had a girl. She just trying to save herself." Dontae shouted before bursting into laughter.

"Boy, whatever. You childish, grow the fuck up!" Chantel blurted before strutting down the stairs.

"I'm glad to see that this shit is funny to you, Dontae!" Skylar couldn't hold back her tears anymore. Dramatically she burst into sobbing, dropping to her knees, covering her face of shame.

"What the hell you crying for? Shit, not even that serious man, for real. Damn, that's why I don't have time for this shit."

"You don't have time for what?" Skylar jumped back up to her feet and charged at Dontae again. This time she missed. He'd ducked quick enough to dodge her blow.

"I don't have time for this shit, this parenting shit. I don't want to be a teen father and you shouldn't want to be a teen mother. We got our whole life ahead of us man. I'm trying to go pro, I can't do that with a child hanging over my head!"

"Really Dontae, so that's how you feel?"

"Yeah, that's how I feel."

"So, why couldn't you just be a man and say that from the beginning then, instead of dodging my calls and shit like a little boy?" Skylar muffled out between her sniffles.

"I am a little boy and you're little girl. We not ready for this shit man!"

"Oh, now you'll a little boy, but your ass wouldn't a little boy when we were fucking now where you?" Skylar fasten the button to her colorful romper that Chantel had snatched apart. Her breast was exposed, and they began to harden from the cool breeze blowing threw the opened windows.

"Man, look, what you're going to do?" Dontae arrogance irritated Skylar's soul. She hated feeling like a burden or like she was begging for something when she wasn't. All she wanted was some support and compassion, something Dontae had promised to give her throughout the entire ordeal.

"You know what? Fuck you, Dontae! You got me all the way fucked up these days. I don't know who you think you are talking to but I'm not the one for the disrespectful shit!"

"How, am I disrespecting you? Tell me that." Skylar threw her hand up and walked away.

"Where are you going? Let's talk!" Dontae blurted out before Skylar slammed the door behind her.

21

Voices babbled continuously like a dripping faucet inside the house. Skylar didn't need to hear the words to know they were talking about her. She waited on the porch for a few seconds to clean the tears from her face and to come up with a descent lie about her disappearance and then barged right into the house through the living room where the worried crowd gathered; Claire, Kerry, Bryan and Shaniya.

"Where the hell you been, Shaniya? And why were you driving my car? You don't have no real license. Those are learning license, Shaniya! You're starting to get more and more reckless every day. I just don't know who you are anymore." As Kerry shouted about, everyone eyes fixated on Skylar. Their faces were stubbornly unimpressed with Skylar's puppy-dog pout. Just second ago, Skylar had believed she could take the heat. She had a solid plan to pretend everything was okay but standing in the mist of the fire proved she couldn't take the pressure; everything wasn't okay. Her world was falling apart right before her eyes and she had no strength to stop it. Skylar tears burst forth like water from a dam, spilling down her face. She could feel the muscles of her chin tremble like a small child as she tried to look away from everyone judging eyes.

"Dontae is cheating on me and he said he doesn't want the baby anymore!" She blurted out before dropping to her knees in the middle of the floor. Everyone who had pre-judged her behavior including Kerry was now embarrassed of their judgements and pissed at Dontae's poor choices. Skylar's body trembled like a branch on a tree. She could barely catch her breathes between the long pauses. Shaniya dropped to her knees to Skylar's side, they were now equal, "Baby sister please stop crying. I promise you, everything is going to be okay. Forget Dontae childish ass. He's going to get what's coming to him, you can believe that."

As comforting as Shaniya's words were supposed to be, they weren't. All Skylar wanted was Dontae's touch, Dontae's support, his comforting; not her aunts or her sister's. Skylar knew her family loved her without a doubt, but it was Dontae's attention and affection she craved. Her eyes dripped with tears. Her walls, the walls that once held her up, had completely collapsed. She was weaker than a cancer patient.

"He doesn't love me anymore..." Skylar cried out. Salty drops fell from her chin, drenching her floral purple, pink and yellow romper. She tightly hugs her tummy with both arms, still she trembled. She couldn't stop though she wanted to. It's raw, everything, raw tears, raw emotions. Skylar had no control her emotions had taken over.

"Why can I not stop crying?" She muffled out.

"Because you're hurt baby." Claire replied to Skylar with a croak in her throat. She was a blink away from tearing up.

"I'll talk to Dontae. His ass is just probably running scared right now. It's actually a normal instinct but once he hears from a man that it's not the end of the world, he'll come to his senses." Bryan said as he hugged Kerry in his arms. He hugged Kerry because he knew better than anyone, when Kerry kids hurt she hurts and though her nieces weren't her biological kids, she never considered them anything less.

"Would you do that for me uncle Bryan?" Skylar asked as she snorted up the snot from dripping down her nose.

"Yes, baby girl, I'm going to talk to him. You have my word, you won't be going through this alone. His ass helped you make this baby, therefor he's going to help and comfort you through this process. Yaw are going to decide what's best for the both of you together." As comforting as Bryan words were, Skylar couldn't see Dontae changing his mind. He'd made his stance clear on the situation.

Skylar slowly stood to her feet and gently broke away from Shaniya's bear hug.

"I'll be fine sister, I just need to go clear my thoughts." Skylar said before dashing up the stairs. Shaniya knew clearing her thoughts meant crying her eyes out until they felled heavy and she was fast to sleep but she didn't argue with Skylar. She knew how it felt to just want to be alone away from peoples and their million questions, their judgements, and their helping hands.

"Just give her some time, her heart is broken right now." Claire said as soon as Skylar was out of sight.

"Poor baby, I can only imagine how she must be feeling." Kerry added as she broke away from Bryan's hug.

"I should go over there and beat his little punk ass. How dare he treat my fucking sister that way!" Anger boiled deep in Shaniya's system, as hot as lava. It churned within, hungry for destruction. Everyone knew Shaniya would do anything for her sister. For it had seemed like to them they were all each other had at one point. The two were thick as thieves. Shaniya could barely take just standing around watching Dontae drag her sister. She wanted to make him feel what Skylar was feeling. The pressure of Shaniya's raging sea of anger forced her to say things she did not mean, "I'll have glock boys knock his ass off or even rob his fucking mother blind of her child support earnings."

"Shaniya, you don't mean that. There are other ways of handling situations like this." Shaniya couldn't hear Claire of her boiling anger.

"His little bitch ass. He not even all that anyway. Little punk ass faggot!" Shaniya paced back and forth as she thought of a plan od destruction for Dontae. Claire knew she had to step in and changed the mood before things grew out of control. It was only going to take Shaniya to recite three more threats before Kerry felt obligated to join her, grandma Claire assumed.

"How about we go get Skylar's favorite; pizza hut and wings. We can even buy those chocolate chip cookies she like and get some scary movies from the Red Box. Who's down?" Claire asked with much excitement.

"That don't sound so bad. That might just cheer Skylar up a little bit, help take her mind of her problems for a while." Kerry replied.

"Shaniya go get Skylar and tell her we're going to make tonight family night in her honor. She'll love that." Shaniya giggled for the first time tonight. She agreed with her aunt Kerry. There was only one thing Skylar loved more than family night and that was pizza and wings.

"Skylar...!" Shaniya yelled out on her way up the stairs.

"Wow, I could've done that." Kerry joked as Shaniya continued to yell out, "Skylar...!" When Skylar didn't answer, Shaniya just let herself into her room, but there was no Skylar, and then Shaniya checked the bathroom. There, Skylar laid flat out on the tile floor unconscious with a pill bottle in her hand.

"Aunt...! Aunt...! Help me...!" Shaniya scream pierced through Kerry's soul. Instantly, she grew chill bumps, her nerves rattled, and her heart dropped into her stomach. Quickly, she dashed up the stairs trailing the sound of Shaniya's horrific screams, "Help me aunt...! She isn't breathing!"

"Ooh my Goodness!" The sight of Skylar unresponsive body stretched out in Shaniya's arms terrified Kerry. She speedily checked Skylar's pulse.

"Good, she got a pulse but it's weak. Call the ambulance Bryan, hurry up!" she yelled out in terror.

Waiting is easier for Bryan and Claire than it is for Kerry and Shaniya. The two paced back and forth as they waited to hear from the doctors. All sort of horrid thoughts flowing through their minds. Picturing life without Skylar was just impossible and very frightening for Shaniya. Skylar was the Ying-to-her-Yang and there was no way she could survive life without both her sister and mother.

"Sit down baby-girl, you're worrying yourself too much." Shaniya took Bryan's advice and finally sat for a few minutes. She tried to empty her mind of the negative thoughts and invite some positive ones. She stared so hard at the walls her mind almost fabricated a dream staring her and Skylar, but Shaniya wouldn't let it happen. She wanted to stay prepared and on her feet. She had to stay woke to reality, for Skylar and not depart into some fantasy.

Waiting for the doctor made Shaniya head hurt. Her head felt like it had taken a beating with a hefty plank of wood and the Tylenol Kerry had given her wasn't working.

"Sorry for the wait..." The doctor appeared like an angel in dream. Quickly, the family jumped up from their seats and rushed the doctor. Kerry who had never sat to start with was front and center. Impatiently, she waited for the doctor to get through all his fancy medical terminology and tell her what was going on.

"So, what does all of that mean? Is my niece okay? Is she going to make it, what? I'm confused dammit!" Gently doctor Bradly placed his hand on Kerry's shoulder and said, "She will be fine. She just needs a large amount of rest."

"And her baby? How is her baby?" Shaniya blurted. Dr. Bradly took a few minutes to respond, Kerry could hear him swallow the room had grown so quiet.

"The baby didn't make it, did it?" Kerry asked shaking her head in disbelief.

"No, the baby didn't survive, I'm sorry." Shaniya was surprised to see the disappointment on her aunt's face, since she had been against Skylar being pregnant from the start.

"Does she know yet?" Shaniya asked.

"Yes, she knows." Dr. Bradly answered.

"Okay, thank you doctor for everything you've done. I'm thankful for your services. Can we go see her now?"

Before Dr. Bradly could answer, the appointed social worker who sat in the cut of the waiting room intervened.

"First, I'll need to talk to you Kerry." It was if she'd been waiting for forever to add her two cents. With her nose tooted and her eye brows raised, Kerry turned to face the heavy-set Caucasian.

"You can talk to me after I see my niece. I don't have time for this shit right now." Kerry snapped.

"This will only take a second, but you can't see Skylar until we talk. So, it's up to you." Shelby snapped back. Kerry rolled her eyes with disgust and then hesitantly walked over to Shelby. As she took a seat next to Shelby, Dontae barged into the waiting room with dramatics, "Is she okay? Where is she?"

"You have the nerve to show your face here!" Shaniya yelled out.

"What you mean, Bryan called me." Dontae snapped back.

"Why would you call him?" Shaniya snapped as she ran up on Bryan like she was ready for 8 round match with him.

"Why wouldn't he call me? That's my baby." Dontae yelled.

"Oh, now it's your baby? But you the main one who was talking about you didn't want no baby and all that shit. You left her deal with this shit alone and now look. You're coward ass bomb!" Shelby watched the drama unfold and instantly she got the answers to her questions.

"So, is this the event that led her to attempt on her life."

"Yes, she had an argument with her boyfriend about the baby and then came home and tried to take her life." Shelby listened attentively to Kerry as she wrote down notes in her pad.

"Okay, it's making sense now. You can go see your niece. I know it must be hard trying to keep up with two teens. I know, I have two girls myself." Kerry didn't bother correcting Shelby, she only had Skylar to think about because Shaniya was grown and off at college, but she just listened and nodded her head, waiting for Shelby to give her the go ahead once more.

"You can go check on Skylar, I'll talk to the sister and give you a call later on for any other information I may need."

"Thank you, Shelby and don't hesitate to give me a call. I'll be ready to answer any questions you have. I just need to get to Skylar right now."

"I understand, go ahead Kerry. I'll call you." Kerry stormed out the room right pass Shaniya and Dontae who were still arguing loud enough for the entire hospital to hear.

"I'm sorry, I didn't mean for her to do this. I just didn't know what to do." Dontae voice carried much guilt, but Shaniya had no sympathy.

"So, you figured you should leave her to figure it out. Like she wasn't fucking scared herself, coward!"

"Okay, Shaniya that is enough." Bryan intervened and said.

"It's never going to be enough. My fucking sister just tried to kill herself because of this nigga and she lost her baby, fuck him. You can feel sorry for him but I'm not!" Shelby wobbled over to Shaniya's side to get a question or two in, "Have your sister ever showed signs of this behavior before"

"Hell, naw she hasn't! She was a happy camper until she met his bullshitting ass."

"So...?" Before Shelby could finish her question, Shaniya blurted out, "Look lady, I don't have time to talk to you, move out my damn way. You want to know what's going on talk to him. He the one with the full details." Shaniya yelled before strutted out the room. Dontae took one shameful look at Shelby and then he broke down to his knees crying. Both Bryan and Shelby consoled him until he was calm enough to tell what happened between he and Skylar.

22

"Girl Dontae took begging to a different level. He was outside last night looking like a little ugly gremlin, crying with rain dripping from his coat. Talking about some, *Please, Shaniya let me see her. I need to see her, I can't sleep at night. I think if I see her my bad dreams will go away.* I said go home Dontae." Kerry could hear the girls, joyful laughter from a mile away, their giggles echoed through the halls and into each and every room in the house. It was at times like these that she was thankful to have a house full of kids. Their laughter warmed her heart. She was glad Shaniya was able to bring Skylar back to life. She remembered her and her big sister Khloe sharing the same tight-bond.

"Skylar, don't you know he broke down like a kid throwing a tantrum in a candy store?"

"Shaniya, no he didn't girl?"

"Yes, he did Skylar. If I'm lying our momma is a bitch. That boy was crying like a little baby."

"I kind of feel sorry for him." Skylar replied before staring off into space.

"Look at me," gently, Shaniya turned Skylar face by her chin. The two gazed into each other's sorrowful eyes, "You have nothing to be sorry about. You did nothing wrong and don't you ever forget that." Slowly, Skylar nodded her head.

"You right, his ass was the one who stirred up all this mess. All he had to do was be honest about his feelings, instead of lying." Skylar blurted as she sat up firmly on the bed, resting her back on the head board.

"Damn right it's his fault! Now, make your next move your best move. The ball is in your court and if I don't know nothing else I know he's learned his lesson. Just don't mess it up by being to soft with him. Stay firm, keep your feet on the ground."

"See, what I'm I going to do without you here sister?" Skylar whined.

"Awe, baby sister I'll be back. You're breaking my heart." Shaniya wailed back. She then leaned in to kiss Skylar on her pouted pink glossy lips.

"I love you and you know I will back before you know it. Besides, me and Khloe don't do nothing but get on your nerves the whole time I'm here anyway, with our loud games." Skylar giggled a little and replied, "Now, that's the truest thing you've said all day."

"I'll see you later chic, Brody outside waiting." Shaniya said as she looked downward trying her hardest not to face Skylar.

"He been waiting for hours too, he probably like, *what the hell is she doing up there?*" Skylar joked but Shaniya couldn't cough up a smile.

"Why you looking so sad, Niya? I'll be okay girl. Go ahead and enjoy yourself. Yaw had this trip planned for a minute now. I'm going to be fine, I promise you." Skylar assured Shaniya.

"I just feel so bad, I shouldn't be going on a trip when you're going through what you're going through." Slowly, Skylar stood up to hug her big sister.

"Bye girl, stop being so dramatic. I told you I'm fine, crybaby."

"Okay, well, I'm going to call you as soon as I make it and I'll tell you all about it later." Tightly, Shaniya hugged on her little sister as she said goodbye with so many tears dripping from her eyes, she could not see. She tried to hide the tears; however, there was such a flood of them that she could not control them.

"Both of our men are going to think we crazy if you go down there crying and what not." Skylar joked as she wiped her sister face dry with her polka dot cotton pajama top.

"And why you got on these tight ass jeans on a road trip?"

"What I supposed to have on, Skylar?"

"A dress, a skirt, anything that makes it easy for you to pee if you have to pull over on the side of the road or if you have to give him a little inspiration to stay up while driving." Both the girls giggled, Shaniya could not believe the girl Skylar was slowly turning into, "Look at you, giving me tricks to use. That doesn't sound so bad though. Too bad I don't have time to change."

"I know we've wasted enough time up here crying." Skylar followed Shaniya out the room, down the stairs and out the front door where everyone including baby Bryan watched her leave.

"Them jeans don't look too bad on you. They are fitting that booty right!" Skylar yelled out as Shaniya jumped into the Ram truck looking like a true college student in her yellow stripe silk blouse, Levi jeans and dusty white All-Stars.

"Bye mommy!"

"Bye Khloe, I love you." Shaniya yelled out the window as she and Brody pulled out the driveway. Khloe, Bryan, Kerry, and Skylar watched the truck until they couldn't see it anymore. It was always hard to say goodbye to Shaniya when she left.

"Come on you, get back in this house and off your feet. You're still on bed rest." Bryan said to Skylar as he waved her into the house.

"I know, I know..." Skylar dragged her feet scrubbing her fluffy yellow house shoes on the floor. She made painful noises when she moved like an elder woman would.

"Are you still having them headaches?" Kerry asked as she watched Skylar wobble up the stairs.

"Yeah, but I just took something for it, so, it should be letting up soon. I'm just going to go lay down for a minute."

"Okay, I'll call you when dinner is ready."

Under blue and sunlit skies, the view was astounding, for the lake teemed with life. To the chorus of birdsong from the surrounding green bushes, and the sound of carp sucking amongst the flowering lily-pads, mother duck, watchful for the predatory pike, scooped the surface for food, with her mini-me's trailing behind like a row of bobbing corks. Dab chicks and coots fed in the safe haven of the reed-beds, whilst flashing green and blue dragonflies hovered above Shaniya and Brody heads.

What Shaniya had assumed would be a little run-down shack was actually a beautiful glass lake house. She finally concluded; Brody parents was loaded. He tried down playing their financial stability, but she had done the math and the numbers determined they were rich or at least well off. Brody stayed with pockets of cash, he drove a brand-new Ram truck off the lot and he didn't have a job. He never not once not had money when Shaniya asked or never have he starved some nights like most the college students did when their parents couldn't help them out for the month. The struggle never hit him and that always made Shaniya curious about Brody's upbringing, but he would never give her full details. Every childhood story was short and to the point. Shaniya figured he was probably just one of those spoiled kids who was never satisfied. He fitted the rich unappreciative kid aura to the tee.

"You haven't really said much since we got here. Are you okay?" Shaniya peacefully inhaled and then exhaled gently as she watched the glistening lake with her sparkling eyes.

"Everything is just so beautiful. I wasn't expecting this."

"I can tell you something else that's beautiful." Brody said as he slid Shaniya over closer to him. The two cozied up on a pallet that Brody had made for them.

"Is that right?" She questioned flashing her beautiful picturesque smile.

"Yelp... You know I think you are the prettiest black girl I ever known." Jokily, Shaniya snapped, "Really, the prettiest black girl? So, am I supposed to be flattered, because right now I'm feeling very much insulted."

"No, it wasn't insult crazy ass girl. It was a compliment. I mean, I get where you are coming from but it's facts. I think you're a beautiful ass black girl. You and your sister and aunt got the dopiest complexion and yaw own that shit. I think that's what makes it so dope." Shaniya totted her lips and mug Brody with her sharp side eye.

"I guess I'll let you slide this time but, I'm not just a beautiful black girl. I'm a beautiful girl period. You put beside any chic, white, Latina or light-skin/black and I'll still be beautiful." Shaniya joked with a serious tone.

"You so damn cocky it's ridiculous. Anyway, take these clothes off, it's hot out here." Shaniya loud laughter echoed and scared the birds from the trees. If there were any neighbors, she would've disturbed them.

"It is not hot out here. Is that the best thing you could come up with to get me out my clothes?" Brody tussled with Shaniya to get her clothes off as she giggled at his desperate measures.

"Oh, you know I don't get tired we can go all night." Brody joked as he continued to try and rip Shaniya clothes from her body.

"What is it going to take?" he asked after failing at his mission.

"All you have to do is ask." She replied with a very seductive tone.

"Shaniya, can you strip for me baby?" Slowly, Shaniya stood to her feet, blocking Brody's view of the lake with her body.

"Sure, I can do that for you. Anything else you want me to do for you baby?" Gently, Shaniya slid the picnic basket filled with fruit and Publix deli fried chicken to the side on the manicured lawn off the pallet. She knew things were about to get freaky and she didn't want to waste the food. Publix had been a long way down the road and by the time she was finished with Brody, she was going to need something to eat and maybe even a cigarette, although she didn't smoke.

"Damn, your body so beautiful." Brody murmured as Shaniya slowly slipped from her blouse, and then her Levi jeans, and then finally her bra and panties.

"You're not afraid someone will see us?" Brody asked as Shaniya gradually moved in closer to his space. Teasing him with her every movement.

"So, let them see us then." Shaniya talked bold because she knew there was no one remotely close enough to see them. There wasn't another house until three-four miles down the road, that's how excluded the area was.

"Oh, I like you like this. I'm about to wear you out." Brody growled before pulling Shaniya in closer to him and flipping on her back. Her breast jiggled like obedient Jell-O as she laid flat on her back, with her legs up anticipating Brody's next move.

"Damn, you so beautiful." Brody said as he stood over Shaniya body impatiently stripping from his jeans. She watched her view with a pleasing smirk on her face, she could barely wait. Her body craved his touch. The scenery was breathtaking, the mood was right, her hormones were high and the Pink Moscato had sluggishly kicked in.

"Baby, how did it get so hard? I haven't even touched you yet?" Shaniya joked. She giggled until she couldn't breathe anymore, but it wasn't at her joke. It was Brody dancing around like a drunk cow-boy slinging his hard penis that had Shaniya tickled to the core. For what seemed like forever, she laughed, that's until she caught a glimpse of a ghost peeking around the tree. Quickly, her smile turned into a frown and her heart sink into her guts. *It can't be... It just can't be*, Shaniya thought as her eyes instantly watered. She swiftly sat up, snatching up her clothes.

"What? What's wrong, what you see?" Brody questioned before he turned and faced the ghost with his penis at attention.

23

Brody's face fell faster than a corpse in cement boots. In that instant his skin had redden, his mouth hung with lips slightly parted and his eyes were as wide as they could stretch. There wasn't even a point in reaching for his pants he had already exposed his jimmy.

"So, this the type of shit you like?" Words left Shaniya. She stared blankly into Wayne dark deadly eyes burning with anger, and her heart fell silent. "Answer me!" he roared. But she couldn't will her lips to move. As if stuck underwater, everything was slow and warbled as he waved the shiny black 9mm around.

"Please don't hurt him Wayne, he has nothing to do with this. It's me you want, just let him go, please!" Arrogantly, Wayne chuckled.

"Well, aint that a bitch for you! She loves the one nigga that betrayed her and betrayed the one man that really loved her." Again, Wayne burst into laughter.

Shaniya chest heaved up and down as she tried to wrap her head around things. If what she was hearing was true, Brody was just as much as her enemy as Wayne.

"You promised you wouldn't hurt her!" Brody blurted out. There is no hint in his voice of his supposed English heritage, he sounds as Jamaican as Wayne do, more so perhaps. Brody had a Jamaican lilt to his voice that had to be passed on from family. Memories of Brody suspicious activities flashed through Shaniya's recollection like lighting. She had quickly remembered everything from Brody pressuring her about opening-up about Wayne to him hesitating to speak about his family. Everything was adding up now, even the large sums of money he carried around. The only time she had ever saw so much in a flesh like that is when she dated Wayne.

"You snake bastard!" Shaniya yelled out with her trembling voice. Wayne couldn't tame himself, he laughed uncontrollably. Things were getting better by the minute for him.

"He paid you to do this to me, didn't he? That's why you always have large sums of cash on you. How could you? You don't know what you've done. This man is dangerous, you fucking idot." Shaniya trembling vocals echoed but there was no one there to hear her.

"Oh, don't worry sweet heart, he knows how dangerous I am. I'm his uncle. There was no coincident in yaw attending the same school." Speechless, Shaniya just shook her head with disgust as Wayne bragged about his perfect revenge. She stared Brody down with her glistening eyes. He could see the pain of the betrayal painted onto her face. If he knew way to fix things he would but there was none. He knew his uncle and Wayne wouldn't stop at nothing to get his revenge. He had waited too patient for this day.

"Where is my child, you little back stabbing whore?" Wayne growled.

"What child? You don't have no child." Shaniya snapped back.

"I told you, she gave her baby up for adoption. She really doesn't have a child." Brody said to Wayne as he began to dress himself. Furious, Wayne began pacing the beautiful manicured lawn as he scratched his head with the tip of the gun barrel.

"I'm so sorry, I had to do it, or he would've killed my sister. I didn't expect to fall in love with you." Brody whispered to Shaniya when he realized Wayne back was turned.

"He doesn't know anything about Khloe. I couldn't dare put her in this." he then whispered even lower before Wayne circled back around to face them.

"I can't believe you nephew."

"I'm telling the truth. I've been to her house and met her family and everything. There was no baby." Shaniya nervously began to dress herself as the two men talked. She held her yellow blouse close to her chest while she wobbled into her Levi jeans with her free hand. She needed to make a run for it while the two argued about trust and betrayal.

"I could you lie to me, I'm your fucking family? Doesn't that shit mean anything to you young motherfuckers?"

"I'm not lying uncle Wayne! I don't know what else you want me to say." Brody sentences sounded repetitious and the pronunciation of some his words ended up being damaged. His accent was as obnoxious to listen to as Wayne's was. Shaniya hated they didn't stress some words enough. How Brody had switched his accent was still so baffling to her, he'd never shown one sign of his accent before running into Wayne and now he was in complete Jamaican mode. It was as if he couldn't wait to be freed to be himself again.

"I didn't betray you, Uncle."

"Did you really think I was going to leave my entire operation in your hands. Do you think you're my only foot soldier? I know all about baby Khloe." Stunned, Brody paused before he spilled another lie. He nervously stared at his uncle as he began to pace the yard once again.

"You broke my heart nephew, you broke my heart. Now, I got to lose my sister and my nephew because there is no way she's going to forgive me for this." Shaniya heart beats increased as walked closer to Brody. Both she and Brody knew what was coming, only she prayed her instincts was wrong. As soon as Wayne raised his arm with the pistol aimed at Brody's head, Brody began pleading, "Please uncle don't do this man, I'm your favorite sister son. I have dreams and goals and so much life to live. Don't this uncle, please!" Without second thought, Wayne pulled the trigger. One bullet to the head and Brody was out. His body propelled backwards crushing the lawn. The bullet wound looked nothing like Shaniya expected from her extensive crime drama viewing on television. Instead of a neat reddened hole it was oozing with dark congealing blood and the putrid smell made her gag reflex. She raised her hand to her mouth and then spied the brain matter on the money green grass beneath his head.

"You see what happens to motherfuckers who betray me, Niya?" Wayne gradually walked towards Shaniya. She couldn't breathe, it felt as if someone was choking her. Her heart was racing and all she wanted to do was curl up into a ball and wait for someone to save her. But no one would, no one was there. A choked cry for help forced itself up her throat, "Help me somebody!" and then she felt a tear drop run down her cheek. It seemed as if this was the end of the road for her. Quickly, she took off running into the house.

Wayne didn't bother running behind her, he knew he had her where he wanted her and there was no where for her to run but what he didn't think about is Shaniya using her phone. As soon as she reached the house she pulled out her phone to call her aunt Kerry but of course like worrisome scene in a horror flick, Kerry didn't answer.

"Aunt it's me Niya. Wayne has found me. I'm at the address I left on the refrigerator. Please, hurry come get me. He just killed Brody."

To save this message, please press one.

Quickly, Shaniya hung up the phone and then dialed 9-11. "9-11 emergency, please hold."

"Shit!" Shaniya mumbled as she silently watched Wayne wiggle the door nob to the room she had barricaded herself in.

"You have two choices Shaniya; surrender yourself to me and I only kill you, or stay in this room until I feel like knocking the door down and force myself in. But if I must force my way in, I'm going to order my man to kill baby Khloe, you decide." Trembling like an unstable branch on a tree, Shaniya decided it was best that she took control of the situation. Wayne had once loved her, and if she could successfully tap into his heart, she could probably save herself and baby Khloe, she thought.

"Okay, I'm coming out Wayne, but can you promise me you'll hear me out before you decide on killing me?" Shaniya yelled with a lump in her throat.

"I promise." Wayne replied as he chuckled loudly.

24

Kerry was cuddled up into the sofa pillows, watching baby Khloe play with her dolls when the unfamiliar ringtone echoed from her purse. The loud noise almost gave her heart attack as she was buried deep into thought, thinking about the beautiful day she had just spent with Derrick. Quickly, she ruffled through her purse for the phone. First, she pulled out her phone that seemingly had three missed calls, and then finally, she found the ringing phone that was clearly Derrick's phone. She stared at his handsome picture on the screensaver for long seconds with a smirk on her face before answering, "house of beauty, this is cutie."

"Oh, I think I have the wrong number. I was trying to locate this man name Derrick's, but I know he not cute, so I must have the wrong number," Derrick joked. Kerry laughed a little and then asked, "How did you leave your phone in my purse Mr.?"

"I don't know, you seem to find a way to kidnap my phone every time I'm around you." Kerry blushed like a school girl, wiggling her toes, "Maybe, I wanted to do a little background check on you. So far I've talked to three of your girlfriends and one baby mama." Derrick deep voice carried sound as he giggled uncontrollably like a teenage boy.

"Well, that's not something I'm worried about. I'm single and I definitely don't have a baby momma." Kerry heart twinkled as she listened to Derrick provide her the assurance she wanted her to hear; he was single and opened to be all hers.

"Well, maybe one day you will have a baby momma." Kerry teased.

"Yeah, whenever you're ready to give me one, I guess." Kerry paused, she couldn't think of the right words to say. In a different life she would have loved to give Derrick kids but she this wasn't a different world and she already had kids and a loving husband to go with them.

"Speaking of kids, where are yours? The house seems so quite." Kerry eyes wandered over to Khloe who hadn't not notice a thing Kerry was doing since she found her favorite doll; the Baby Alive doll.

"Oh, my son is with his daddy and Skylar is Gods knows where, so, it's just me and baby Khloe but she hasn't been stun me since she found this little creepy doll."

"Let me guess, the one that does all the things a real baby do?" Derrick asked.

"Yelp, that's the one."

"I saw that shit on TV and man, that shit creeped me out. All I could think about is Chucky." The littlest things Derrick did and said tickled Kerry. Her loud outburst startled Khloe. She quickly turned around to see what had her aunt laughing so hard.

"I know right... I didn't think about him. I'm telling you, if this damn doll start doing anything suspicious, I'm going to set it on fire." Khloe gripped her baby tight, and said to her aunt, "You can't set baby Liyah on fire, she hasn't been bad aunt."

"Oooh, you're going to jail for cruelty to children." Derrick joked.

"Shut up, I'm taking you down as an accomplice." Kerry murmured to Derrick before turning her attention back to Khloe, "Baby I wasn't talking about your baby. I'm on the phone. I know baby Liyah is a good baby like you."

"Oh, you so smooth..." Derrick said.

"Shut up Derrick, you are getting me and trouble. And come get this phone before I call all your girls and tell them you got me pregnant." Kerry whispered into the phone, making sure Khloe didn't hear anything she could repeat around Bryan.

"I'm on the way love, do I need to bring my pistol? Is ole boy there?"

"No, I told you he's gone. Just hurry up and come get your phone, man." Kerry end the call before Derrick could respond. She knew how that drove him crazy. She giggled at her pettiness and then reached over to the coffee table to grab her sub that Khloe was eyeing. Kerry mouth watered, she could smell the bacon, mustard and vinegar. She'd had the sandwich for at least an hour, but she wasn't hungry, suddenly, she was ready to demolish the sub.

"Here, you want some?" Kerry said to baby Khloe as she broke her a piece of the sandwich. Just as she was shoving the sandwich into her mouth the door bell rang.

"Oh, I know he is not here already?" Kerry mumbled as she quickly wiped her mouth of the food crumbs and then ironed the wrinkles out her plaid black and red romper.

"Who is it?" she yelled out.

"It's me, who else?" Derrick shouted back. Forcefully, Kerry slung open the door and questioned, "How the hell did you get here so fast?"

"I didn't too long just drop you off. I hadn't gotten that far."

"That was a minute ago, Derrick."

"Anyway, Kerry where is the phone?" Derrick snapped.

"What's the rush?" Kerry asked as she twist her butt down the hall dramatically, knowing Derrick was watching her.

"Aunt, I want more." Khloe said as soon as Kerry entered the living room.

"There is no more, Khloe. I'll have to make you one." Derrick chuckled startled Kerry, she noticed he'd followed her into the living room.

"I asked your stubborn butt if you were hungry, you said no, but you two in here trying to get full off that one little sandwich that I told you wouldn't full you up."

"I wasn't hungry at the time, thank you. Neither was she, so…"

"So, what?" Derrick said as he pushed up on Kerry from behind.

"Woman lets go get something to eat. My treat, this baby hungry." Derrick murmured into Kerry's ears before plotting a wet kiss on her neck.

"Stop, crazy." Kerry pushed away from Derrick and reached into her purse to grab his phone.

"Khloe put your shoes on, we're going to get some McDonalds." Excited, baby Khloe quickly jumped up from the floor and ran out the living room to get her shoes.

"Oh, you'll big spender, I like... I like." Kerry teased as she slid on her gold between the toe's sandals.

"Oh yeah, I take care of my women." Derrick joked back before pushing up on Kerry again.

"Will you stop before my niece sees you?" Kerry mouth said one thing, but her actions said another. As Derrick cuddled her up in his arms, she hesitantly and gently kissed on his neck.

"Come on, let's hurry up before ole boy pop-up. I'll hate to have to kick his ass in his own house."

"Um, excuse me? You will not be kicking nobody ass around here, thank you." Kerry tossed her purse on her shoulders as she followed Derrick to the front door.

"Khloe, we're leaving!" Kerry sang out. Speedily, Khloe came running to the door with her baby doll in one hand and her mini purse in the other.

"We ready, we ready," she sang out while jumping up and down.

"Well, com on baby." Derrick scooped Khloe up in his arms and took her the car. The two waited patiently for Kerry as she locked up the house. When she finally, buckled in, she noticed Derrick had scrapped Khloe down in a car seat.

"When did you get a car seat. That wasn't just in here when we last saw you?" Kerry asked. Derrick could see the worried-curiosity mug painted on her face, so he changed the tone with a little joke, "I had to go to my baby momma house and get the baby after you called her and told her about us." And just like Kerry was back laughing.

"Oh, my bad I didn't mean to get you in trouble." Kerry replied as she scuffled through her purse for her phone.

"Damn, did I leave my phone?" she mumbled as she continued to ram shack her purse, pulling out personal items like Always pads, lipstick, and peaches and mango bath and bodywork lotion.

"What you need a phone for? You're with me and baby Khloe today." Kerry didn't stop her mission, nor did she find Derrick charm attractive at the moment. She grew more frustrated by the seconds.

"I forgot my niece called me, and she left a voicemail. She doesn't usually leave voicemails."

"She's a big girl, quick treating her like she's a kid." Derrick snapped. His tone had changed from jokingly into selfish and irritable in a matter of seconds. The noticeable change made Kerry stop looking for her phone, and instantly she turned her attention towards Derrick.

"What you say?" she questioned with a conspicuous attitude. There was something puzzling in Derrick's manner, enough to send Kerry's hand into her purse, holding on tightly to the pepper spray on her key chain. It was like something was weighing on his mind and suddenly he looked demonic in the eyes.

"You heard me loud and clear Kerry." Derrick never turned to face Kerry, his eyes fixated on the road as he talked, and Kerry's hand continued to roam in her purse. She didn't bother replying to Derrick, it was clear to her that his mood had changed for the worse. So, she quietly searched for her phone, and then finally, there it was tucked under her Maybelline make-up kit. She quickly pulled it out her purse to redial Shaniya's number but before she could say, *Hello*, Derrick had quickly reached over and clocked her in the head with his fist, knocking her out cold.

25

Hating Dontae was like a snake eating its own tail, or worse. It hurt Skylar more than it hurt him and it just kept going around and round. Everyone kept telling Skylar that the pain would pass with time, that she'll move on when she found someone new. She wanted to believe them but then she didn't. The larger part of her still loved Dontae and he was who she wanted to be with, still after all they had been through. Only, she wasn't going to let him know her true feelings until she felt he'd suffered enough for his wrong doing.

Skylar knew after Tim she would never be the same girl anymore; her purity and naivety had died. She envied those that marry their childhood sweethearts, the ones that never felt the keen sting of betrayal. For a short while she believed that would be her and Dontae but the anguish of forming a strong bond with him, to only have him rip pieces from her still beating heart changed things for the worse. It was an invisible wound that would take a lot of time to treat. Skylar had plans to forgive and move on, but she planned to move with caution.

"I know you hate me Skylar, but you got to forgive me one day." Skylar listened to Dontae beg as she walked the bare street kicking an empty Sprite bottle like a soccer ball. The wind howled like some horror movie opener and the sky was dark as bats, but Skylar worried about none of that. She needed a breath a fresh air, time away from everyone at the house, and she wanted to talk to Dontae without fear of being spied on.

"I know I have to forgive you, and I have, for my sake but what you did want just go away because you said sorry Dontae."

"I know Skylar, and I don't expect it to. Trust me, I know we got a lot to work on and I'm willing to put in the work, but you got to work with a nigga here. I fucked up and I have admitted to my wrong but damn, I've been begging you for how long now?"

"I don't know, I haven't been watching time. I've only being trying to keep afloat. You know, keep my mind clear and free of negative thoughts."

"Yeah, I get that. I know it must be hard for you right now, man, damn, I hate this shit." Silently, Skylar placed her hand over her mouth to giggle a little bit. She was enjoying every bit of Dontae begging and pleading. It felt good to hear him beat himself up over her suicide attempt, to her it meant he cared for her. Which was great because for a minute of her life, she believed he didn't.

"Baby we're going to get through this shit and I promise you, when the time is right, we're going to make another baby and this time I'm going to be right by your side, the whole time. I can never put through this type of shit again and that's facts." Skylar paused, she didn't respond to Dontae, but it wasn't because she didn't believe him or know what to say. The stranger behind her had caught her full attention. His shadows grew closer and closer. The faster she walked, the nearer the shadows grew.

"Skylar, you there?" Dontae asked calmly. The baritone of his voice rumbled through Skylar's bones and rattled her nerve.

"Yes, I'm here, hold on. I think I'm being followed." She dramatically murmured into the phone. Dontae jumped up from his bed and then yelled into the phone, "Where the fuck is you? I'm about to meet you now!" The loud roar of his voice was comforting, and Skylar was sure now, more than ever that Dontae loved her.

"I think he's gone now, I don't see him." Skylar searched for the mysterious shadow, but it was gone. Not a soul in sight.

"Where are you?" Dontae questioned.

"I'm fine, I think it was just someone passing." He squeaked and then flushed lightly when he realized that Skylar was just being paranoid. "I'm fine." she repeated.

"You just being paranoid. Take your ass home man." Dontae chuckle was soft and rolling like thunder that billowed across the dark skies on a stormy night.

"I'm on my way..." Skylar sentence was cut short and her next jumbled up words echoed as she strained to scream for help through the rough hands that covered her mouth.

"Help me!" she managed to yell after the biting the stranger's hand.

"Skylar!" Dontae yelled back. He could hear her mumbling for help in the back ground. It was clear to him that her mouth was covered.

"Fuck!" he blurted out as he quickly stepped into his wheat Tim boots and rushed out the front door. He didn't know where to drive to, but he assumed Skylar wasn't far from home, so he was going to start there.

"Stop yelling, dammit!" The stranger demanded before he knocked Skylar out cold with one blow to the head and threw her in the back of his trunk. When Skylar waken, she found herself chained to a chair. Other than the noise of the generator, the room was a silent concrete box. It could be anywhere. Skylar swiveled her neck for a window, there was none. For all she knew she could be deep underground, in some random room in an isolated prison or in someone's personal cell.

Above the only source of light was an old-fashioned bulb on a bare white wire and its switch was nowhere to be seen. There was something amateurish about the way the concrete walls had been set. The angles weren't quite right and there was a roughness to the texture. That in itself ruled out quite a lot of places and potential abductors. Skylar money was on this being someone's personal homemade jail cell and that could either be far preferable or very, very bad. When heard the footsteps, her dropped to her stomach and her anxiety increased. Who could possibly want to hurt her and what was they going to do to her was the questions Skylar wanted answers to as she patiently waited for the stranger to reveal himself. His footsteps grew closer and then, he flicked on the light switch.

The dim light had temporarily blinded Skylar but when she gained her sight back, she was surprised to see that Shaniya's old flame, Khloe's daddy, Chance had been her abductor.

"Chance?" She blurted out with confusion.

26

Seduction was what Chante did best, moving into Bryan's personal space with just the right look of heat in her eyes. She didn't just look at a man, she looked into him as if she knew his desires. Bryan smiled, playing it cool, knowing full well that Chante was about to seduce him. She softly rubbed the top of his hand and his lungs expanded with briny air.

"Your hands are so strong but they're soft at the same time." Chante voice had the accent he knew so well - her words were soft and sexy. It was the same tone the girls at the office used when they wanted to ask Bryan out. Chante seductive tone paired up with the smile that already played on her face, told Bryan to run. He was in for trouble if he didn't find a detour quick. Speedily, he dived into his bag for one of his law books to hide behind. He could stare at the text, act like he had something better to do than talk. Then he could go back to thinking about his new case, the facts weren't adding up. There was so much to research and get right.

"Can you not work for just one minute please?" Bryan let the book sink back into his bag, he needed another diversion. He could just tell Chante to bag off, but he didn't want to hurt her feelings, she was an old friend or make her mad. She could easily start trouble with him and Kerry.

"Oh, I'm sorry to bore you. This case got me swamped. I could call you tomorrow when the paper work gets faxed in. That way you don't have to wait. Once you signed the paperwork I'll be out your hair and you can go on with your excited little life." Chante giggled a little and then plopped up on Bryan's desk. His eyes gawked over her body, adding up her pluses and minuses like a mathematical equation. If he had to rank her, she would make a A+, a straight out hundred. There was nothing not perfect on her; legs, breast, smile, waist. Chante had the whole package, only she wasn't Kerry and Bryan loved his wife.

"You're not a bore to me silly." Chante, in one smooth motion turned so that she was straddling Bryan, her little black dress riding up her thighs ever so slightly. Their gaze lasted a full second, enough for each to take in the face of the other. Nothing needed to be said, at least that's what Chante believed. Her repeated aggressive actions had already taken care of the message.

"Chante?" Bryan whispered between heavy breathes. His manhood had begun to rise and slowly he was slipping into dangerous territory.

"Let's just allow her bodies to communicate, we don't need words." Chante replied as she gently grabbed a hand full of Bryans dick into her hand.

"How about we don't." Bryan snapped before lifting Chante up off him and onto his desk.

"What? What's the problem?" Chante blurted with confusion painted onto her face.

"You know what's the problem, Chante."

"I see the way you look at me, Bryan." Chante walked over to Bryan, cornering him to the wall.

"Can you honestly tell me you don't want me?" Gently, Chante rubbed Bryan chest through his crisp white button-down shirt. She looked into his eyes and she could see the desire sparkling with fire. It had always been written in their gaze, a chemistry, a seed of love, an invitation to learn about the other. Even when they were accompanied with a crowd, they stood apart, hearts beating all the faster when a chance to talk came.

"Today is our day. We may never get this day again." As convincing as Chante was, Bryan knew better. He knew a few minutes of lust wasn't worth the lifetime of grief he would cause Kerry.

"I'm sorry for leading you on, Chante. I can admit to craving your touch. I mean what man wouldn't, you're beautiful. No, scratch that, you're perfect, but I got a wife and I love her too much to betray her this way. I promised her there was nothing going on between us and I don't want to break my promise." As hard as it was for Bryan to break free of the lock Chante had on him, he did. He pushed her from his personal space and speedily walked over to his bag where his phone rang.

"Hello?" he answered with his very shaky and husky voice.

"Somebody got her man, this shit fucked up! I can't find her nowhere. I'm swear I'm going to kill me a nigga on God!" Dontae voice was filled with utter rage, cursing not-loudly, spewing out slang. Bryan couldn't understand his words, he only knew they were curse words for the taut tone of Dontae's voice, because his words sounded strangely tuneful, is was like he was rapping. They were rhythmic but venomous, like a freestyler on a Brooklyn corner.

"Calm down, I can't understand what you are saying. This Dontae, right?"

"Yeah, this Dontae! Where you at? I can't get in touch with Kerry. I guess she still tripping on me or some shit but she not answering her phone, neither is Shaniya."

"I'm at the office. Calm down, I can't hear with all the yelling. What's going on?" Chante watched Bryan attentively with wide eyes and lurk ears. She wanted to know just as bad as Bryan what was going on.

"Somebody got her man, somebody just swooped up and got her!"

"Somebody got who, Dontae?"

"Man, are listening to me or what bruh? Who else I'm going to be calling about? Somebody got Skylar!" Dontae shouted into the phone.

"Somebody got Skylar?" "How do you know, when, where?" Bryan questioned.

"We were on the phone and she was walking home for whatever reason and somebody snatched up! I been circling yaw block for a minute now, but I don't see nobody. I called the police too, I'm at your house but nobody is here."

"I'm on the way, stay where you at!" Quickly, Bryan swooped up his grey leather brief case and zoomed out the door. He was so in tuned to Dontae, he completely forgot about Chante. She waited for a minute to see if Bryan would double back into the office to tell her bye and explain why he had to go but he never doubled back, so she quietly slipped out the office. She avoided being seen. She'd endured enough embarrassment for one night.

"I was on the phone with her, you know talking about getting back together or what not and then all of a sudden, she got silent. I asked her what was going on, who she saw but she said whoever it was must have gone because she didn't see them no more, and then boom! Somebody just scoops her up. I could hear her screaming for help in the back ground. It was like he had his hand over her mouth or something!" Dontae paced back and forth in the yard as he explained to the cops what had happened. He'd tried his best to avoid profanity like Bryan asked but it was hard. He was craving to scream out FUCK, like smokers craved nicotine from a cigarette.

"How do you know it was a man?" The officer asked as he scribbled in his notepad.

"I don't know it was a man. I just it was, because whoever it was had to have strength to just scoop her like that. She would've fought a woman. She not a scary bitch, she'll fight in a minute." Dontae talked with his hands like he was rapping his favorite lyrics.

"I understand," the officer replied before walking off to call in a report on his walkie-talkie.

"This shit is fucked up man!" Dontae turned to Bryan to say.

"Yeah, I know." Dontae looked at Bryan and observed his calmness. Something was adding up right he thought and as soon as the policemen where gone, he was going to check him about it.

"Where going to police the neighborhood and little further. We put out alert. As soon as we have news we're going to contact you. I know asking you to wait patient is asking a lot but trust we're going to do everything we can to find her." The policemen shook Bryan's and Dontae's hand and then jumped into their cars, speeding out with the sirens on.

"Aye man why are you so calm?" Dontae turned ask Bryan.

"Because I think I might have a clue who have her and if I'm right, it's nothing a deputy can do for me. I got to call in some big shots. Kerry's not answering her phone, and neither is Shaniya, so, I'm almost positive I know who's behind this." Closely, Dontae followed Bryan into the house. He wanted to know more but it was clear Bryan wasn't trying to be heard by the nosey neighbors who were all out standing around gawking their every move.

27

Bullets whizzed over Shaniya's head as she ran away from Wayne and his hit squad, they were deep, twelve to her one. Adrenaline coursed through her system as a fight or flight instinct. Her survival skills had kicked in right after Wayne made it clear he didn't care to hear about her reasons to betray him. Shaniya figured Wayne was going to kill her whether she stayed or ran, so, why not try to fight to stay alive. It was a better option than just waving the white flag.

Shaniya knew she would never out run Wayne and his crew, it was too many of them. But if she could make it to the black van the men pulled up in, it was hope she could possibly live. She looked back, breathless, checking their distance. They were closing in. Coming from all angles of the house. She had to make it to the van, and quick. Shaniya saw out the corner of her eyes as one of the men was almost close enough to make a grab for her. She turned around blasting the pepper spray Brody had given her and the goon fell over screaming and clawing at his eyes. She turned back around almost too late to see a motorbike racing towards her. The rider had taken a grab at her, pulling on her yellow and white blouse but Shaniya jerked away stripping the blouse from her body. Finally, she reached the van, but she fumbled with his keys she'd taken from the goon that was driving after she tased him. A hail of bullets rocked the van, puncturing the side and the gas tank.

"Shit!" She blurted before she quickly moved away from the van. In moments the van exploded, engulfed in an inferno of orange flame. With the van burned her hope of escaping. There was no way she was going to get away from Wayne now, but then she quickly thought, the van burning could be a gift within a curse. If someone saw the van burning they would most likely call for help. Now, all she had to do was stall time.

"I give, you win!" She cried out as she slowly walked from behind the large tree decorated in the front yard.

"I told you I was sorry. I never meant to hurt you Wayne. I was young, and I was scared. I didn't know Johnathan was a cop and I definitely didn't know he was there to destroy your operation. All I do know is, I'm tired of running from you. I'm tired of being scared. So, if its my destiny to die tonight then, so be it." Tears dripped from Shaniya watery eyes as she slowly walked towards Wayne who'd put his hand up moments ago to stop the reign of fire.

"Bring her to me!" Wayne demanded. Speedily, the strongest man out the crew snatched Shaniya up and toted her to the front door where Wayne stood.

"Put this fire out." He said the goon before turning to Shaniya and demanding, "Follow me."

"What are you going to do to me Wayne? What do you want from me?" Shaniya cried out as Wayne shut the room door behind them.

"I can't change the past. I've apologized, what else can I do to fix this? I never meant to hurt you, I promise I didn't!" Wayne cornered Shaniya to the wall, not a smile in sight. His mouth a straight line, a mysterious darkness in his eyes. He moved in so close she could feel his breath on her face. Adrenaline flooded her system once again like it was on an intravenous drip - right into her blood at full pelt. If felt as if Shaniya's heart would explode. She wanted to quell the hammering in her chest, but there was no way.

The anticipation had her anxiety at a high. She'd wished Wayne said something or got the torture over with at once or was that his plan all along; to keep her guessing of the punishment?

After staring into her soul for long moments at a time with his cagy eyes, he broke his gaze and finally uttered just one word, "Undress." Shaniya's anxiety decreased just a little, *Oh, so you're going to rape me*, she thought as she began to undress slowly.

"Don't do this, Wayne." Shaniya whimpered as she slowly slid her pants down her curvy petite hips. Shaniya didn't have much to take off since her shirt had already been ripped from her body.

"What, I'm not good enough to have you but my nephew is?"

"No, it's not like that, Wayne and you know it." Shaniya replied with tears dripping from her glossy eyes.

"Shut up, quick crying, and stand up and present yourself to me." Wayne demanded with a simple calm tone. He swept Shaniya's hair behind her ear and kissed her neck hard, pushing her back against the wall. Shaniya's insides went cold. This was nothing like the times she'd willing given herself to Wayne. He wasn't the funny man who told jokes over the music, he wasn't the gentle man who held her hand in public, or the man who used to hate to see her cry anymore, he was now the demon from hell. She froze as he began to remove her nude padded bra.

"No!" Shaniya pushed against Wayne chest. He moved his head back to meet her eyes and then said, "Either this or die." Shaniya tears increased but she was no longer fighting. Khloe was all she could think of. She needed to live so that Wayne could never get to her.

"If you ever loved me, now is your time to show me." Wayne growled into Shaniya's ear before biting down on it.

"I did love you Wayne," Shaniya sobbed before Wayne throwed her onto the bed. Sexing him was like watching paint dry but she pretended to be in tuned for the sake of mending fences with Wayne. She secretly hoped he would spare her life afterwards, at least long enough until help arrived.

28

Wayne slept like a baby, Shaniya sex had him out cold. It was the perfect time for her to run, but where would she run to? The goons guarded the door with their lives and Wayne slept with his pistol in his hand. His phone was tucked away in his back pocket and he laid on his back. Shaniya knew if she'd made the wrong move, he would wake up agitated like a sleeping veteran. A sleeping paranoid criminal could easily kill on the spot, accidently. So, Shaniya figured her best option was behaving, and probably, just maybe she'll gain his trust.

Shaniya watched television to pass time by, but she didn't know what she was watching. She didn't laugh when she was supposed to, she didn't feel any tension during the drama, she barely followed the plot. She just sat there next to the Oreo packet until to her surprise they were gone. Then she tapped out the crumbs into her palm and threw her head back to inhale them. Her eyes rested back on the flickering screen and found that in her brief distraction the commercials had begun. They were short, attention grabbing and required no intellectual effort. Once they were over her mind turned to the chips in the cupboard. She crunched on the *Salt & Vinegar* chips staring back at the flickering TV and then suddenly, the loud munching had woken Wayne. His tap on the shoulder startled Shaniya.

"Give me the remote, I got something for us to watch." He said. Hesitantly, Shaniya passed Wayne the remote. She really wasn't up to Netflix and chilling with her rapist.

"There isn't a movie in the DVD player," Shaniya said when she noticed Wayne trying to switch from cable channels to HDMI1.

"Oh, I don't need a DVD. This Bluetooth capability. We're going to watch something off my phone." Irritably, Shaniya rolled her eyes while fixating her attention on the television. She couldn't bare to look at him. Wayne gawked at Shaniya as he hit 'play' on the recording. He didn't want to miss her reaction. He expected a loud outburst, and some file words but Shaniya didn't say anything. For a long moment she stared at the television. Her mouth remained an uncharacteristic grim line, almost robotically. Her eyes were almost as still as some bill board poster. She couldn't believe she had put her aunt in danger.

Tears dripped from her eyes as she watched Derrick man handle her aunt. He forcefully threw her onto the bed and ripped her clothes from her body. Kerry tussled with him, but his strength out powered hers of course. Shaniya turned, but too slowly to be normal. When she spoke her voice trailed slowly, like her words were unwilling to take flight. There was a sadness in her eyes, the brown was very glossy.

"Please, make him stop Wayne. It's me you want, it's me who betrayed you. Can you just get your revenge with me and leave my family out of it?" Wayne giggled with an arrogant smirk on his face.

"No sweat heart, that's not how this works. When you betray a man like me, everybody you love pays the price. Do you think I don't know Khloe isn't mines? One look at that baby, was all I needed to confirm that bit of information. So, not only did you bring down my entire operation, and have me arrested but you cheated on me."

Again, Wayne giggled. His arrogance was like spit to Shaniya's soul. She felt so violated, vulnerable and disrespected.

"What kind of man enjoy seeing a woman get rape? I don't even know how I lasted with you as long as I did. And you call yourself a man. I could've sworn you had some sort of morals about yourself when we first met. I opened up to you about my past, just for you to turn around and use it against me. You have someone kidnap my aunt and rap her! You're not a man, you're a coward!" Shaniya words hit Wayne where it hurts. He once cherished her opinion and he still valued what she thought about him.

"Shut up and watch the damn TV, little whore!" Aggressively, Wayne turned Shaniya's face to the television and stationed her head in one place with his hands.

"It looks like she is enjoying it to me," Wayne said before bursting into laughter. Shaniya blood pressure increased as Derrick forcefully shoved himself in and out of Kerry. She wanted to kill Wayne, but she had no weapon, and not enough courage.

Kerry numb face sank Shaniya's heart. She watched her aunt endure the abuse with tears dripping from her eyes. Derrick slid his tongue dip into Kerry's ear. His roughed fingers curled in her hair. Every time Kerry closed her eyes he bashed her head backward onto the bed demanding she open them. She didn't want to, she closed them over and over, she'd rather see dark than watch his face light up with power and lust as he forced his way deep into her guts.

Just as he whispered into her ear, "I'm about nut." Kerry swiftly took the knife she'd stolen from the kitchen from under the pillow and buried it into his stomach right to the hilt. The knife met his flesh, soft and pudgy, and it made a satisfying squish as the tip of the blade sank deep enough to make Derrick scream. Kerry twisted the blade in her hands, all the while sinking it deeper and deeper. Her skin was tearing to shreds as the knife rotated, the sound of his muscles and nerves being gouged grew louder. Then, without warning, Kerry jerked the knife all the way into Derrick gut, until the shiny metal had disappeared inside him and the black handle was pushing against his broken skin. His cry was most satisfying to Kerry, a brilliant sound, guttural chokes mixed with an agonized roar. Kerry smirked like a mass murderer and pulled the blade out of Derrick. She looked at his stupid surprised eyes and giggled a little. She shoved him as he rolled to one side, she'd been trapped beneath his body ten minutes too long.

"This bitch is crazy," Wayne murmured as he watched Kerry murder his best friend like he was a new comer to the game. His dick surprisingly rose, poking out from his briefs. Kerry demonic look had given him a different type of feeling. A lustful crave he wasn't to familiar with.

"I'm on my way to you Shaniya. Just hold on baby girl!" Kerry looked and yelled into the camera. Her boldness had triggered Wayne anger all over again and quickly he pointed his pistol to Shaniya's head.

"Do you think your aunt got wings to get here quick enough to save you bitch!"

29

"Wayne, calm down please!" Shaniya blurted as she fearfully took a few steps backwards tripping over the remote in the floor.

"You're such a weak bitch! I had no business giving you my heart. All I've done for you and this is how you repay me?" Wayne eyes burned with fire, and his rage frighten Shaniya. He'd suddenly grown angrier with her then he'd been the entire night.

"Why are you so angry with me now, all of sudden? I thought you were going to give me a second chance Wayne. A chance to prove my loyalty to you?" Shaniya cried out. Wayne waved his pistol around carelessly like it was a toy gun. If he had no real intentions to kill Shaniya, he could still easily kill her mistakenly. Shaniya brain had shut down. She was clammy and there was the glisten of a cold sweat. She'd ran out of ideas to convince Wayne to spare her life and it had seemed he had run out of patience to listening.

"Shut up, Bitch! I'm tired of hearing you run your fucking mouth." Speedily, Wayne charged Shaniya with his gun, pointing it directly to her skull.

"Any last words bitch?" Shaniya watery eyes enlarged and the hairs on the nape of her neck bristled. A gaggle of goose pimples laminated her frigid, naked skin. Slow and deliberate, Wayne clicked the pistol off safety. She tried to scream, but the inside of her mouth lacked any moisture and a croak was all that issued from her gape. Finally, the sound she'd fearfully anticipated resonated.

The gunshot cracked into the air as loud as thunder but without the raw power of a storm. In comparison it was tinny and small. Shaniya badly wanted to mistake the gunshot for the cracks of an oncoming squall, but she knew there wasn't a cloud in the sky, *I'm shot*, she thought as she dreadfully patted her body.

Where did he shoot me, why aren't I burning? Maybe, I've gone into shock, and the pain will come later. She believed before being deafen by another gunshot. Her senses sharpened with adrenaline, Shaniya held her breath, before looking down at her gut where she believed she been hit, but there was nothing. Not a whole in sight. "I'm not shot," she concluded. Quickly, Shaniya noticed it was Wayne who'd been shot instead of her. He'd been hit in the chest, propelling him backward in an awkward cartwheel. Slowly, Wayne fell onto the floor. For a few seconds he looked up at the ceiling as if he was trying to pray God before closing his eyes.

"Wayne?" Shaniya blurted out before dropping to her knees by his side. She stared at his lifeless body confused. She'd closed her eyes right before the gunshots sang so she wasn't quite sure how Wayne had been shot and not her. Suspiciously, she looked around the room, straining to hear with every ounce of her concentration. The room was silent again. The only sound was the cool air that whispered through the shattered window. Then suddenly, Shaniya figured it out. *The shots came through the window. Wayne gun was never fired.* She picked up his piece and true enough it was cold as steel.

Slowly, Shaniya crawled over to the window for a view. "Ahhh!" she screamed frantically, as Chance appeared from the shadows.

"Shaniya, it's okay. It's me, Chance." Broken glass splattered onto the floor and outside on the ground as Chance lift the window to climb in. Shaniya had quickly gathered her nerves and finally, she exhaled. She wasn't sure how and why Chance was there, but she'd never been happier to see his face.

"Shhh, they might hear you." Shaniya whispered to Chance as she turned her attention towards the door where Wayne goons were posted.

"There is no one alive to hear us, they're all dead. You're safe now, it's okay." Chance replied as he pulled Shaniya in to comfort her in his arms. He looked like a thief in the night. Dressed in all black everything, Gloves, mask, clothes and combat boots. It was clear he was prepared for war, and to be prepared for war, he had to know it was coming. Rapidly, Shaniya jerked back, pulling away from Chance grip.

"Wait, how did you know I was here? How, did you know Wayne was here? What's going on Chance. Why are you here?" Shaniya heart beats increased as her suspicion of Chance amplified. Hurriedly, she scooped up Wayne's gun from the floor.

"Calm down, Shaniya. Let me explain everything before you go jumping to conclusions."

"Explain, I'm listening!" She demanded as she aimed the gun towards Chance head.

"I've been following you ever since I found out Wayne had been released from prison. I knew he would be looking for you, so I've been staking out in the shadows, watching your every move." Slowly, Chance stepped towards Shaniya with his hands out. He could tell she wasn't digesting the information well. Confusion was painted all over her face.

"Step back, don't take another step! So, it was you following me around at the school, and not Wayne?"

"Yes, and no. He'd sent some guns to your dorm to kill you but when the man killed your roommate instead, he'd come up with the idea to torture you. Originally, Brody was supposed to kill you, but he couldn't find himself to do it. So, Wayne made him bring you hear so that he could do it himself." Shaniya heard Chance and she even believed him, but it was just too much for her take in. She began to pace the floor, dropping her arms and the gun. Speedily, Chance picked up the gun, and then rushed over to hug Shaniya tightly.

"I know it's a lot, but you are finally safe now. He can never hurt you again." Again, Shaniya snatched away from Chance bear hug, and loudly she blurted, "Oh, shit! My aunt, I need to call my aunt and see if she is safe and if Khloe is safe. Oh, shit and Skylar too!" Shaniya panickily searched the room for Wayne's phone.

"It's okay, Shaniya! Everybody is okay. I kidnapped Skylar and hid her so Wayne goons wouldn't get to her like he instructed. Khloe and Kerry are okay too. I talked to her, she killed the goon that had betrayed her as well. Everybody is safe, I promise you."

"I can't believe I watched my aunt kill someone. She's so gangster." Shaniya joked as her nerves relaxed once again.

"You saw that?"

"Yes, Wayne thought it was a good idea for me to watch him rape her, but quickly the tables turned when she killed him. Suddenly, he got angrier and wanted to kill me fast."

"Yeah, that was his best friend, Derrick."

"Oh, that explains the sudden anger." Shaniya said.

"I don't know how to think you Chance. I really don't, but I hope you didn't miss any step because I want this life behind me. I can't take this leaving in fear any longer."

"You don't have to worry baby, everything is good. Your life is yours again." Shaniya plopped down onto the bed and began to dress herself. She smelled like sex and wore few clothes. She was too scared to get dress why Wayne was sleep out of fear of waking him.

"So, you just covered all angles, didn't you, captain-save-a-whore?" Chance giggled a little as he attentively watched Shaniya slide the Levi jeans up her beautiful curves.

"Well, you know how I feel about you Shaniya and don't say that about yourself. You're not a whore. You was a young girl who was manipulated at a very vulnerable moment in her life, that's all."

"No, I don't know how you feel about me, Chance. You left me and your baby behind." Shaniya snapped.

"No, you stayed behind. I never left you, anyway, we're not about to get into all that right now. There are a million bodies laying around here. We need to leave. Let me get you home to your family first, and then we'll talk about all that."

"You still bossy I see." Shaniya replied as she followed him closely out the house.

THREE MONTHS LATER...

Kerry could feel the fear in her chest waiting to take over. Perhaps it only wanted to protect her but there really wasn't any danger. It sat there like an angry ball propelling her towards an anxiety she just didn't need. She shyly turned away from Bryan as he kneeled on one knee.

"Bryan, what are you doing?" Kerry managed to croak up before the tears began dripping down her powdered cheeks. "I'm making it right again." Bryan replied with much in his heart. He appeared before Kerry, in all his grandeur. A tailored black suit with a charming black tie. His chiseled jaw lifted with a proud, pleasant smile. His eyes a sparkling charcoal, so much like his fathers, and his soft, wavy-like black hair complimented his thick black brows. He was charming and smart. His voice was that of any rich boy, honeyed and proud, "Kerry, my sweet love, will you marry me, again?" Kerry was overwhelmed with emotions and she could barely breath, let along talk, so, she shook her head instead and finally Bryan was relieved. He couldn't bare spending another day without her. For three months, Kerry had been torturing herself for the foolish decisions she'd made. *How could she be so stupid and flirt with temptation, when she had such a loving husband like Bryan*, she thought. For many nights she cried, thinking about her decisions and how they could've of cost her everything. Kerry was so upset with herself, she asked Bryan for space and maybe even a divorce if she couldn't get herself together.

Though he'd accept her apology long ago, she just couldn't forgive herself. She constantly thought about how she treated Bryan and how she'd accused him of changing and cheating when in reality it was her playing with fire and changing with the seasons. For three months she pushed Bryan away and smothered the kids. She wouldn't let the girls nor the babies out of her sight. She'd promised their mother, her sister that she would keep them safe and she was determined to keep her promise.

"You don't know how happy you've made me today Kerry." Anxiously, Bryan placed the new and upgraded five carat diamond ring onto Kerry's finger.

"I thought I lost you." He whispered into her ear once he'd stood to his feet, wrapping her tightly in his arms. The party guest cheered as the two rocked side-to-side in each other's arm.

"You're my soulmate woman, I'm not trying to do this life without you." Kerry blushed a little and replied, "Today I'm happy, but I don't think you can really tell. It's under the surface and mixed with my anxiety. I'm not used to the combination, it's truly odd. Happy takes me up and anxious brings me down, so in that combination I'm simply focused on the task at hand and that's enjoying the moment, but Bryan I want you to know my emotions are a part of me, and in this relationship, they blend with yours in the most delicious of ways.

Yet there are times I have storms inside, never because of you, and it's important that you understand that, but from the damage, the triggers of my past. I want you to know that the fear comes from another place and time, that there is no connection to you. It is for me to remember that you love me as much as I love you. And then in those moments of storm I must find my calm core by myself, center myself, or else I will always need to be calmed. I love you too much to do that to you, so from this day forward, I promise to keep on learning, keep on evolving, and maturing. Then I will become the wife and friend you deserve, able to give love freely, completely." Bryan could tell Kerry spoke from the heart, and knowing she was ready and willing to put in effort to make their marriage work, warmed his heart.

"We got this. We're going to be in this thang for a lifetime, believe that!" Bryan shouted out to the guest as he rose the champagne glass he took from the waiter tray. He'd called all his and Kerry's closet friends out to help them celebrate their wedding anniversary. The celebration was a riot of color, everyone a little more hyped up than they should be. Kerry's eyes ate up the scene like a post Ramadan feast, her limbs felt supercharged and her head giddy. Everything about the flowing silks tailored to her body made her want to dance, her feet moving with grace and her heart beating with joy. Finally, her family was free, and clear of the drama, lies, and grief. It was finally time for the black butterflies to live at peace, and one with life.

Shaniya had finally accepted Chance fifty apology, after he'd explained a hundred times that he wasn't really with the woman and child she'd saw him with at the fair.

"I'm going to believe you this time, but I still think you was at that fair with that woman." Shaniya nagged as she and Chance dance like long time lovers on the floor.

"Baby, the only woman I want is you. It's been that way, since I met you. I can't lie, I thought I could get over you and live life without, but I quickly discovered I couldn't. So, here I am, back at your grace. Please God be my shepherd," he joked. Shaniya jabbed him in the arm with her fist and replied, "Ooh, you got jokes I see."

"I'm just joking, I'm the happiest now that I'm with you and my baby girl." Skylar looked over at Chance and teased, "Awe, that's so cheesy. Don't yaw sound like a little old happy couple."

"Look here youngster, you don't know nothing about this love right here. You and little Thugger over there got a lot of growing to do before you can get to this level."

"Oh, we not that young now, don't do that." Dontae added. He and Skylar was the only two twerking and swagging at the upscale Great Gatsby ball theme party.

"Just look at how yaw dancing." Chance burst into laughter at Shaniya's joke. A couple of years back, Shaniya would've been Skylar, twerking about and Skylar would've been ducked off into a corner somewhere, but times had changed drastically.

"Hey, I'm sure they twerked back in the day in their ball gowns too." Skylar added before she dipped down again in front of Dontae's manhood and began dry humping him with her round Georgia peach. The celebration went on into the night, everyone dancing like they'd forgotten how to stand still. Skylar was moving like she'd been working at Magic City for years. Her butt clapped like a professional stripper. Shaniya watched her little sister with a proud smile painted onto her face. Skylar had finally jumped out her skin, and finally, she was fully confident in her beauty and the clear of the quality's she brought to the table.

Kerry's face resembled Shaniya's, as she scoped the scene. It was an epic picture of pure excitement. She'd finally build the family she and Khloe dreamt of having. She knew in her heart, that her big sister Khloe was proud of her and that brought much joy to her heart. Finally, they were living their best life!!!!

THE END

Maybe, ⁇ Would you like to see a spinoff with Chance & Shaniya, & Dontae & Skylar? If so, comment "Spinoff" in the review section on Amazon. & as always, thanks for the continued support Butterflies... Goodbye----Until next time!

Made in United States
Orlando, FL
04 March 2023